FALLING FOR THE NANNY

KAY KNOLLS

Falling For The Nanny

Copyright © 2022 by Kay Knolls.

All rights reserved. Except as permitted under the U.S. Copyright Act of 1976, no part of this publication may be reproduced, distributed, or transmitted in any form or by any electronic or mechanical means, including information storage and retrieval systems, without written permission from the author, except for the use of brief quotations in a book review.

This is a work of fiction. Names, characters, places and incidents either are the product of the author's imagination or are used fictitiously, and any resemblance to actual persons, living or dead, business establishments, events, or locales is entirely coincidental.

ISBN: 979-8-9852093-2-7 (E-book)

ISBN: 979-8-3531825-3-5 (Paperback)

Editor: Kristen Womble, Passkey LLC.

Copy Editor: Zainab M., Heart Full of Reads.

Cover Design: Shari Ryan, MadHat Studios.

Find out more about the author and upcoming books online at www.kayknolls.com

ACKNOWLEDGMENTS

A HUGE thank you to my wonderful editor, Kristen Womble at Passkey Publishing. Your expertise and invaluable insights help me tell the best story I can. I am grateful.

A special thank you to my copy editor, Zainab M. at Heart Full of Reads. Thank you for polishing my grammar so it shines.

And THANK YOU! to you my dear readers. Thank you for taking the time to read my story. I appreciate you!

Dedicated to everyone who decided not to settle for only a piece of the bone. #goodbones

CHAPTER 1

HOPE

Would Johnathan notice if I stabbed myself in the eye with my butter knife?

Would he care?

I reached for my wineglass as I watched Johnathan fire off instructions to the person on the other end of his cell phone. I wondered if Johnathan's poor assistant had ever thought of stabbing him with a letter opener during one of his tirades, just to make it stop. Wait a minute, why was I suddenly pre-occupied with thoughts of violent stabbings? I sipped from my still full glass of white wine, determined to remedy that situation.

"Well, why not?" Johnathan bellowed.

I sunk deeper into my chair, glancing around to see if anyone was staring. Yep, people were staring.

Bartholomew's on the Bayou was exclusive enough that most people who came here came for romance, not business. At eight on a Friday night, the tables were filled with couples enjoying a romantic candlelight dinner for two. Like me, they could do without the power powwow going down at my table. I caught enough pointed stares to know no one was enjoying Johnathan's meltdown.

I opened my mouth to suggest that we could leave if he needed to when he yanked the phone away from his ear and stabbed the screen a few times with his index finger. I would have laughed if I didn't know doing so would only make things worse. Johnathan was way too close to the edge to take me laughing at him.

Before either one of us could speak, Johnathan's phone rang again. He glanced at the screen. The frown on his face disappeared, and the color in his cheeks retreated. He answered; a genuine smile flirting across his lips. The hairs on the back of my neck stood up even as the alcohol pitched in my stomach.

"Janice, this is a pleasant surprise."

I didn't hear her response, but Johnathan's throaty laughter made me want to punch him.

"No, not at all. How can I help?" He reached for his wine, sipping as he listened to her as if he had all the time in the world. As if we weren't in the middle of a dinner date.

Just like that, I knew. This, whatever we had, was over. Three months with Johnathan, and I felt confident that there were no pieces of him that I didn't know. And I didn't like most all the pieces I did know. It was time to admit it and move on. Watching the pleasure on Johnathan's face and the relaxed, unhurried way in which he listened to the woman on the phone, I also had a sinking feeling in my stomach. He was cheating on me with his co-worker, Janice.

It would explain why three months into our relationship, there was absolutely no passion on his part for me. I might as well be a bug in his soup for all the romantic attention he paid me most of the time. I should discuss it with Allie.

Except, she and I didn't talk about our sex life. Besides, she had been the one to introduce me to Johnathan. I had the feeling she would be on his side. Still, I did often overhear Allie and Hydra chatting about their boyfriends when I walked into the teacher's lounge, and they enjoyed passion in their relationships. And by passion, I meant sex. Lots of it.

The girls would be shocked to find out that Johnathan and I had yet to do the horizontal mambo. Apart from kissing that often led to touching before frizzing into nothing, we had yet to take the next step.

In the beginning, it had been my fault. I hadn't wanted to move too fast with him, so I had shut him down when he tried to initiate more between us. I thought I would get to the point where his kisses and touches made me want more. Instead, we'd fallen into a predictable routine of Friday night dinner dates that led to heavy petting back at my apartment, until he pulled away, leaving me with a peck on my cheek at my door, before climbing into his car and driving away. No passion.

Yet, listening to Johnathan's low timbre, seeing the light in his eyes, yeah, I was certain he was involved in some kind of a relationship with Janice that went beyond the workplace.

Besides, Janice was also his boss's daughter, and it was exactly the sort of dick-move a career-driven man like Johnathan would make if he thought it would help him get ahead at his law firm. So, where did that leave me?

I picked up my handbag, and as quietly as possible, I pushed my chair back and stood. Johnathan glanced at me, but I made a dismissive hand gesture that I hoped he would interpret as me meaning that he shouldn't pay me any attention. He averted his eyes again, focusing on his phone conversation. I heard his laugh as I walked away.

Growing up, my mom always said if the foundation was good, everything else would work itself out.

"Good bones, Hope. They'll hold you up when times get tough."

I pushed open the front door of the restaurant and stepped into Houston's hot September night. Johnathan and I did not have good bones. Sure, we were a beautiful couple. We looked good on the outside. He was tall, muscular, and gorgeous like a Viking, and I was short and curvy, with long black hair. I wasn't bombshell material, but I'd been told I was beautiful enough that I never second-guessed my attractiveness. Johnathan, on the other hand, was model material. The fact he was a lawyer and probably spent more hours at his desk than was healthy didn't stop him from working out six days a week at his gym. He was as physically handsome as he was mentally intelligent. If looks were all I was going for, Johnathan would be perfect.

But I wanted more. I wanted someone who was strong but full of grace and kind. I wanted caring and protective. Decisive, yes, but also thoughtful, loving. *Honoring.*

After our blind date, Johnathan had seemed like the perfect guy. I'd thought for sure we'd been right for each other. He'd made it easy to say yes to another dinner date, and another after that. We'd been dating for a month before the cracks begun to appear. Now, three months into our relationship, time had revealed the truth about us. We weren't a good fit.

"Ms. Martinez?" I turned at the sound of my name and found myself standing in front of a familiar-looking blonde woman and a very tall, very serious-looking man. Little Peter Peyton's mom and dad.

"Hi! Mr. And Mrs. Peyton. What a pleasant surprise."

"How nice to see you. Peter's going to be over the moon when I tell him we saw his favorite teacher tonight."

"Aw, how is he doing? Enjoying the weekend?"

"More like counting the seconds until he's back in your classroom."

I laughed and allowed the warm feeling of approval to settle my breaking heart. I loved my job as a teacher. In this moment, knowing that I'd just walked away from a relationship that I'd hoped would go somewhere, I needed the reminder that I still had my life's passion.

"Well, please give him a hug for me, and let him know that I can't wait to see him in class on Monday."

We chatted for a moment before a cab pulled to a stop at the curb. I said my goodbyes and climbed into the back seat. I turned to watch out the back window as Alice and Shawn Peyton walked arm in arm into Bartholomew's on the Bayou. They had good bones. It was evident in the way they touched each other, supported each other, looked at each other with complete understanding and agreement as if they were silently communicating. It was in the way Mr. Peyton wrapped his arm around his wife, pulling her close as he escorted her into the restaurant.

I was pretty sure he would never ignore her for half the dinner while he took a phone call with his assistant and then with his co-worker. Those two knew how to make each other feel special. That's what I was looking for.

I wanted it all: the husband, the love, the children. Why had I settled? Turned a blind eye for so long to the fact that Johnathan and I were on different wavelengths. Who said I had to settle? Determination uncurled itself in my stomach and rose up my spine, straightening it. I wasn't going to settle. I was going to hold out for what I wanted, no matter how long it took. I would no longer compromise just because I was lonely. Good bones. I was going to wait for it. I owed it to myself.

CHAPTER 2

DARIUS

"No offense, Darius, but Shawn sure picked a fine time to grow a conscience."

I looked up at my two business partners who were also poring over documents on the long table in our conference room. Hayden scowled at me, his jaw tense, his lips pressed firmly together. He was right, but I bit my tongue to hold back my agreement.

Shawn was my older brother, and my loyalty was always to him, even when he'd left us up a creek with no paddle. Besides, I knew how hard he was fighting for his marriage.

"Cut him some slack, okay? It's his wedding anniversary, for God's sake. What was he supposed to do? Cancel his dinner plans with Alice?"

"Why not? Hell, it's what I would do."

"Yeah, and that's why you're twice divorced," I shot back at Hayden. "Look, it doesn't matter. He's not here. So, let's just focus and do what we got to do, so we can all get out of here sometime tonight."

"Agreed!" Brian turned his page forcefully and continued reading. Project financing was Shawn's area, but Brian had always been Shawn's second pair of eyes. Tonight, it was Brian's job to double-check we had enough documentation to prove our financial capacity, and the overall feasibility of our project.

Hayden frowned at the map in his hands before setting it aside and hammering on his laptop keys. Thankfully, he remained silent. I needed his complete focus on double-checking the site constraints and our plans to eliminate or circumvent them. As Gemini's lead architect, I'd created the site plan, and I was 99.9 percent sure that I had accounted for everything.

This latest Gemini acquisition was going to make or break us. We were days away from presenting our best offer for the large piece of abandoned land on the outskirts of town that we intended to turn into Houston's premiere shopping and residential area. Making sure we had all our T's crossed and our I's dotted meant combing through zoning and land use documents, examining city codes, surveys and, of course, our financials. Shawn was better at this sort of thing and had a knack for directing Hayden, Brian, and me about what we needed to pay attention to. But he was off on a dinner date with his wife.

I took a deep breath and let the anxiety go. Of course, I understood why he'd done it. I wasn't an expert in the romance department, but it was a foregone conclusion that you didn't ditch your wife for business on your fifth wedding anniversary. Not if you wanted your marriage to last, anyway. But we had a lot of money riding on Project Resilience. It was our most ambitious deal to date. We'd already spent months evaluating the site's potential and comparing our surveys and results to the seller's. We were getting ready to sink over ninety percent of our liquid assets into this deal. We were taking a risk that would leave us strapped for cash. One mistake and we were over. One missed detail, one false step, a miscalculation, and it could mean the end of Gemini Inc. We needed all eyes on this deal, checking and double-checking, that we weren't missing anything before we made that purchase offer.

I probably would have done like Hayden and put off the fancy dinner at Bartholomew's. Shawn had been insistent that tonight he couldn't, and wouldn't, work late. Alice would come first above every dollar we stood to gain, or lose, if this thing went sideways. Part of me admired him for his decision. It was one our father hadn't made, and we'd both seen the effects of it firsthand. The other part of me that was driven to succeed wondered again at the wisdom in Shawn splitting his focus. It seemed like someone, or something, always got the shorter end of the stick. Situations like these reminded me of why I was single. I was just too driven to succeed in business. It wouldn't be fair to the woman. Gemini Inc. simply couldn't afford anything else but our undivided attention and complete commitment. And truth be told, I was okay with that.

Shawn hadn't been tonight, however. He'd adamantly insisted that it wouldn't be Alice doing the sacrificing tonight. So, logically, that meant the three of us had drawn the shorter straw. So here we were, at the office, sitting here past ten at night, scrutinizing these papers.

My phone beeped. I glanced at the screen and saw my mother's name there. Why was she calling me, and so late at night? I answered before she hung up.

"Mother, what's going on?"

"Darius." She paused. After a sharp indrawn breath, she

continued, "Darius, your brother has had an accident. You need to come quickly. We're at Mass Memorial on Fannin."

"Shawn?" What was she talking about? "Shawn's out to dinner with Alice."

"Alice…" She gasped for air. "Alice is dead and Shawn's in surgery. The doctors aren't sure he'll make it. Please get here as soon as you can."

The room tilted and the ground beneath me split wide open, swallowing me whole and spitting me out again. The dial tone vibrated loudly in my ear. She'd hung up. I stared at the phone in my hand, waiting for the answers to come. The only thing that came was a cold sensation of dread spreading down my chest and through my abs. I jumped to my feet, racing for the door.

"What is it?" Hayden called out. He and Brian were already on their feet, coming after me.

"Shawn's been in an accident."

"I'll drive," Brian said immediately, and I could only nod.

Alice was dead. My vision blurred, and I shut my eyes. Told myself to breathe. I didn't dare utter those words out loud. Pain the likes of which I'd never known lanced through my body. Brian pushed the elevator button for the parking garage. I leaned against the side paneling, finding support there. My God! How would Shawn and little Pete survive her loss? I didn't even want to think about it.

I wasn't aware of the ride to Mass Memorial General Hospital. We walked through the front doors and straight to the front desk. A pretty brunette looked up as we approached the desk.

"I'm looking for Shawn Peyton. He's in surgery."

"Are you relatives?"

"His brothers."

"Third floor. Take the elevator up and check in at the desk upstairs."

Moments later, we were stepping off the elevator on the third floor. I spotted my mother slouching in a chair next to a window. Silent tears tracked down her cheeks. Had I ever seen her cry before? I walked over to her, grabbing her hand and sinking into the chair next to hers. She looked across at me with a blank expression on her face. My heart wrenched, as if a piece of me were being ripped away.

"Where is he?"

She shook her head and turned to look out the window again.

Shawn was gone.

The guy who'd taught me how to tie my shoes, brought me my first cologne, and showed me how to shave was gone. My big brother, my business partner, and the rock of Gemini Inc. was dead. And so was Alice. They'd died together. Now, all that was left was Pete.

Gut-wrenching sobbing filled my ears. It took me a moment to realize the sound was coming from me. I stuffed my knuckles in my mouth, bit hard, and fought to breathe. I felt my friends' hands on my shoulders, holding me. This wasn't how we'd planned it. We were supposed to be hotshot developers stacking up billions and growing old together. Passing Gemini Inc. to the next generation. Now the only thing left of my brother was his son, Peter.

Oh my God! Peter! He was at home with the nanny, probably already asleep, expecting his parents to be there when he woke up in the morning. Only, they were never coming back. He was alone!

No, he wasn't! He had me. He was my nephew. Mine to care for, protect, love, just as my brother had loved me. It wasn't what I had expected, but it was what I would do. For Shawn's sake.

CHAPTER 3

HOPE

THREE MONTHS LATER

I hit the ignore button, sending Johnathan's call to voicemail, before I set my phone down on my desk, and turned my attention back to picking up confetti off the wooden floors around my desk area.

Christmas Break had come to Silsbee Academy, and it had started with a bang! A real one, thanks to little Michael's piñata, which he'd brought to the end-of-year party as a surprise for his classmates. We all had fun wracking the poor thing to pieces. The kids had picked up all the candy — but none of the shredded pieces of paper — off the floor. The candies were probably all in my students' little tummies by now. I could leave the litter for the cleaners, but truthfully, I was avoiding packing up my desk and heading home to my empty apartment, where I would spend the next four weeks alone, until classes began in January.

You could always go home.

Yeah, no, I didn't think so.

I dismissed the thought as soon as I had it. Moving in with my parents for the holidays wasn't an option for me. My mom would love to have me sleeping under her roof again, and it would be great to hang out with Dad. But I didn't want to see glimpses of her disappointment and worry over me and my single status. I was twenty-six years old with no prospects. The bad part about my situation was that I wasn't happy about my love life, and it showed. Staying with my mom and dad for the Christmas break, in my current state, would be like waving a red flag in front of a bull. Just plain stupid.

So, here I was, hanging back in my classroom rather than heading home to my small one-bedroom apartment. I pulled myself to my feet and walked over to the trash can across the room. Truth be told, I was lonely. So very lonely. Three months ago, I'd had a boyfriend and been out on a date. Three months ago, Alice and Shawn Peyton had shown me what being in love looked like. Then they'd died tragically in a car accident. That night, as I'd said goodbye to them, I'd promised myself I would not settle. Alice and Shawn Peyton's deaths just made me more determined to not compromise on love and the type of relationship I wanted.

Not for the first time, I thought of little Peter. I wondered how he was doing. Was he liking his new school? His new teacher? I missed the way he would run up to me and hug my legs. Or laugh at the funny books I read. His smile often made me smile, and I missed it. I prayed he was all right. I couldn't imagine what losing his parents had done to him. Kids were supposed to be resilient, right? I prayed Peter was doing okay.

"Ms. Martinez?"

I jumped as the sound of a deep baritone, calling my name, filled the empty classroom. I turned and found myself face to face with a mature, masculine version of the little boy who had suddenly filled my thoughts.

"Mr. Peyton?"

He nodded, taking a step into the room. "Yes. I wasn't sure you would remember me."

I thought back to the last time I'd seen Darius Peyton, standing at the foot of two coffins at a graveside. The shadows under his eyes, the stubble on his cheeks and jaw, even the hard prominent cheekbones told me he wasn't far removed from that devastated man who'd stood with silent tears pouring down his cheeks.

I'd watched him standing alone near their coffins, with so much loss in front of him, and the sight had broken my heart. I'd watched him for a long while, waiting for him to turn and walk away. But he'd stood there, long after everyone else had left, except for the two men who'd stood close by a tree, watching him as well, waiting for him. I'd approached him when it became obvious he wasn't leaving the gravesite soon.

"I remember," I whispered.

He took another step into the room, closing the distance between us.

"I do too. Did you mean what you said?" he asked me now, pulling me away from my memories of the funeral. The low timbre of his voice stroked my spine and had me stepping closer to him.

"That if there was anything I could do to help you and Peter, you shouldn't hesitate to ask me?"

"Yes."

It had been a desperate invitation spoken to that broken

man. A weightless offer that didn't come close to offering the comfort I'd wanted to give.

The last three months had done little to heal Darius Peyton. He looked like he was still standing at his brother's gravesite.

"Yes, I meant it."

I walked over to the small desk and chair and, sitting down, I pointed at the chair next to me. I saw the slight hesitation a moment before he gingerly sat in the chair, his knees brushing against the top of the desk.

"I'm sorry, perhaps you should sit in my chair?"

A smile tugged at the corners of his mouth. "Too late. I think I'm stuck."

Laughter escaped my lips. I slapped a hand over my mouth to stifle it. I felt the heat rising over my torso, my neck, my cheeks. It felt wrong laughing in his presence.

"I'm sorry."

"Don't be." He paused a moment, then continued, "You have a beautiful laugh. That's actually why I'm here."

I shifted my butt in the hard, kid-sized chair, waiting for him to clarify.

"Pete's having a hard time right now. It's expected, of course. But I remember he used to talk about you a lot. In fact, just the mention of your name used to make him smile. You were one of his favorite people."

I watched the sadness spread across his face. I bit my tongue to stifle the impulse to reach for his hand.

"Not much makes him smile these days."

Shoot! Forget propriety. I placed my hand over his, closing my palm over his clenched fists. His hands were huge, warm, hard yet soft to touch.

"I'm so sorry," I whispered.

He took a steadying breath. Then he covered my hand with one of his, holding my hand in place over his.

"Pete's therapist thinks it would be a good idea if he and I both began moving back into our routine. She's hoping Pete will be ready for school in January, and I need to get back to work myself. My business partners are about ready to send in search and rescue. I've been working from home as best as I can, so I can be with Pete twenty-four-seven, but we're about to break ground on a very important project in January and I need to be more hands-on now."

"Has Peter been out of school this whole time?"

He stiffened. I tightened my hand over his hand, holding him in place when he would have pulled away. "I'm sorry, I didn't mean to sound judgy. It's just I hadn't realized Pete had withdrawn so much."

"Some days, it was tough just getting him out of bed."

"I'm sorry. I hadn't realized."

"Look, Peter could stay in bed for a year and I'd be fine with it. He's four years old, and he's lost the two most important people to him. Life blindsided him. He gets a pass for as long as he needs it. But I'm facing a lot of pressure to get back to the office. I need to make sure he's okay while I'm gone."

"Of course. How can I help?"

"Would you consider being his nanny for the next few weeks until I can find someone more permanent?"

Shock had me sitting back in the tiny chair. Now, it was Darius who held my hand in place when I would have pulled it away.

"His nanny?"

"Only until the start of the new year when the agency can find me someone permanent. I dragged my feet on filling out the application, and now it seems everyone's already on an assignment for the Christmas break. I know how much Peter cares for you, and I think your presence might actually help him."

Across the room, my phone buzzed on my desk. A quick glance at my watch confirmed it was Johnathan. Again. I sent the call to voicemail and then focused on the man in front of me and the request he was making.

Could I do it? Could I watch little Peter while Darius went to work? It would be better than my current day plans. Eat ice-cream in bed and binge watch the entire Netflix library or spend time with a little boy who, truth be told, I really loved teaching. It seemed like an easy pick to me. What would it mean for Peter, though? Would he be open to hanging out with me?

"I would love to help. In any way, I can."

Darius sighed his relief. He caressed the top of my hand with his and then looked down at our entangled hands. As if just realizing that we were touching each other, he pulled his hand away and folded them in his lap.

"Would you be able to start tomorrow?"

My phone buzzed again on my desk. This time, I didn't even glance at my watch.

"Do you need to get that?"

"No." I shook my head. I wasn't the least bit curious as to why Johnathon had been blowing up my phone all day. I'd made the right decision ending things with him, even if I was lonely as hell.

"Yes," I answered the question he'd asked me before Johnathan's call. "I can start tomorrow. What time would you like me there?"

He ran his hand through his too long, black hair, but the lock that teased his forehead fell back into place, undisturbed. "Is eight okay? It would give us some time together with Peter before I have to head into the office."

"Sure, eight's fine. I'm usually up at five to make it here by seven. Where do you live, by the way?"

"McKnight Grove."

"Oh." I'd heard about the prestigious gated community where the homes started in the millions, and most of Houston's famous and — infamous — lived.

"Is that going to be a problem for you, transportation wise?"

"No, not unless there's a ban on twenty-year-old Camrys in the neighborhood."

His lips twitched, and I saw the beginnings of a smile. "No, I don't think Derek's implemented that yet."

"Derek as in Derek McKnight?"

He nodded.

He was on a first-name basis with billionaire bachelor, Derek McKnight. Oh crap!

"Where do you live?"

"Out in Spring."

He nodded. "It's a bit of a commute for you. Will that be a problem?"

Forty-five minutes one way. More if there was traffic. "No, not at all."

He seemed to relax a bit, his shoulders dropping from his ears.

"May I ask what do you do for a living?"

"I'm a real estate developer."

"Got it."

"In terms of compensation, is there an amount you have in mind? I'm willing to pay anything."

"Oh, I hadn't thought of you paying me to watch Peter."

"Of course I would pay you. Your time is valuable. What do you make here?"

For the second time since I'd sat down with Darius, I felt heat rising across my skin. Darius was most likely a very rich man. Would he find the little salary I made as a teacher pathetic? Johnathan had.

"It's just watching Peter for a few hours a day. I would have sat in my apartment and done nothing anyway."

"I hope you'll do more than just watch him. You'll need to prepare his meals and keep him entertained. He's missed some schooling, but he's only four and I figure there's plenty of opportunity for him to catch up. However, since you've also been his teacher, it wouldn't hurt if you also tutored him a bit while you two are together. So, why don't I pay you what you would make here? Do they pay you guys well here? They charged my brother an arm and a leg in tuition, so I hope some of that went to you."

"Do you always say what's on your mind?"

"Life's short," he said with a straight face.

It was. Bitterly so. Silence hung between us again.

"I'll pay you ten thousand for the four weeks."

"That's too much!"

"It'll do then."

I watched as he extracted himself, a lot more gracefully than I would have, from the desk and chair and stretched slightly before holding out his hand to me. Instinctively, I put my hand in his and allowed him to pull me out of the kiddie seat. He towered over me. My head barely came to the top of his chest. This close, I could see the green flecks in his golden-brown eyes and the light dusting of gray hair at the side of his temples.

"Next time, I'll try your chair."

I laughed out loud, and this time, I didn't feel guilty about it.

"See you tomorrow, Ms. Martinez."

"Please, call me Hope."

He smiled. "I will."

I watched him walk out of my classroom as quickly as he'd come. Hurrying over to my desk, I scooped up the knick-knacks I wanted to keep safe and then tossed everything into my tote. I grabbed my cellphone and my coat off the hook and hurried out of the classroom. I didn't dread heading home anymore. In fact, I felt anticipation and excitement coursing through me. Suddenly, the looming holidays didn't seem so bad. I couldn't wait for tomorrow to see Peter and his handsome uncle, again.

CHAPTER 4

DARIUS

"Come on, Bud, just try to eat a little of it. I have a surprise coming in a few minutes, and I know you'll want a full stomach for this."

I tried one more time to get Peter down to the kitchen to eat a little of the scrambled eggs and toast I'd prepared for him.

Hope would be here any minute now, and I really wanted us to make a good first impression. I had talked my nephew into getting out of bed and brushing his teeth, but Peter had zero interest in eating. Instead, he sat on his bedroom floor with his Lego blocks spread out in front of him. He was putting the Lego construction pieces together like a boss, and I felt a moment of pride. Perhaps Peter had inherited his father's knack for building things. Now, if only I could get him to eat the breakfast I'd made for him.

I was so in over my head! Despite Shawn and Alice giving me full custody of Peter in their will, I'd still had to argue with my mother for custody of Peter, convincing her that at this stage in her life, the last thing she wanted was a small child. Lucky for me, my father had shown zero interest in Peter living with them, making it easier for her to acquiesce. But I was as bad off as she would have been raising Peter on my own. I didn't know the first thing about parenting a child. It was Shawn who had cared for me. He might have only been four years older than me, but he'd been the closest thing to a parent to me. What had I been thinking when I'd agreed to take care of Peter?

Honestly, I'd been trying to spare my nephew the same childhood Shawn and I had endured. One filled with hired help and absentee parents. But this was hard, and more often than not I felt like I was messing it up. It helped to ask what would Shawn do as I navigated caring for his son. It seemed to help Peter when I approached situations the way I knew my older brother would have. Problem was, I couldn't remember Shawn ever having to coax me into eating.

The doorbell rang. Peter's head popped up, and his eyes met mine across the room. I saw the hope in his eyes a second before his mouth turned down and he looked away. He added another block to the structure in just the wrong position so that the whole thing toppled over. Standing up, he walked over to his bed. Without a glance in my direction, he pulled the covers down on the bed I'd just made and, climbing in, pulled them over his head, shutting me and the rest of the world out.

"Shit," I muttered, not caring about the promise I'd made to Alice the day Peter was born that I would quit swearing until he was eighteen.

This wasn't the first impression I'd wanted to make on Hope, but it was the reality she was walking into. Best not to sugarcoat things for her. She would have her work cut out caring for Peter during the day.

I opened my front door and felt a rush of pleasure race along my spine at the sight of her. She was beautiful in hip-hugging jeans and a white sweater. Her blackish-brown hair fell in loose waves down her shoulders. I felt the heavy stirring in my pants. Wow, I hadn't felt that in months. Three, to be exact.

"Hi." She smiled.

She smelled like wildflowers and some type of fruit. Delicious. She was beautiful in a sweet, wholesome, non-intimating way. She wasn't the glamorously dressed, leggy business woman type I would have dated three months ago. But then none of those women would be here, willing to watch a four-year-old so I could get back to work.

"Did you find us okay?"

"I did. Thanks for leaving word at the security fort up the street that I was coming. I suspect they let me in only because my name was on the list."

A smile stretched across my lips. "Yeah, we're serious about our security around here. Come on in."

I stepped aside to let her into my home. Her eyes dash around the grand foyer before rolling upward to the ceiling. She whistled as she turned in a circle.

"I see why. This is a burglar's dream."

Her sparkling eyes met mine. Her gaze was magnetic, pulling me toward her, and I realized that I'd stepped closer to her. I cleared my throat and massaged the knot of tension forming at the nape of my neck.

"Where's Peter?" She glanced around the foyer one more time, confirming that we were indeed alone.

"We're having a rough morning, I'm afraid. He's up and dressed. Well, he was until he realized it wasn't his mom and dad at the front door."

Her smile disappeared from her pretty lips. "Oh, I'm sorry."

"No, I'm sorry. I shouldn't have said that."

"No, I want you to be open with me. I want to know what Peter's been feeling. It'll help me navigate our time together. I'm not his therapist, but I imagine there's only one way to handle grief, and that's going through it. I want to be as sensitive to him as I can be. To you too." She held out her hand, and I held on to it tight. It felt good to be in physical contact with someone. I hadn't realized how much I'd missed an adult's touch.

"Why don't we go see him together?"

"Sounds like a plan." I smiled and, still holding her hand, I led her up the curving wooden staircase to the second floor.

"Nice game room," Hope said when we got to the top of the stairs and walked by the open space where I'd placed my pool table, fuzee ball machine, and basketball arcade.

"Thanks."

It had been months since I'd used the room. Months since I'd felt like shooting pool with the guys. An image of Hope wearing tight jeans, with a stick in her hand, leaning over the table as she lined up her shot, filled my mind and had desire shooting to my groin.

I cleared my throat, backing away from the game room.

"His room's this way."

I led her down the hallway on the right and stopped at one of the first doors.

When I opened his bedroom door, Peter was still huddling under the covers.

"Peter, there's someone here to see you."

He shoved the covers down and sat up.

"Ms. Martinez?"

"Hi, Peter."

He burst into tears. The pain of it caused my vision to blur. I wiped my eyes and dried my fingers on my pants. Hope walked over to the bed and pulled the little boy close for a hug. He tightened his little arms around her neck and sobbed into her shoulder.

"Mom and Dad went to heaven."

"I know, Peter. I'm so sorry."

I left them there, pulling the door shut behind me. Retreating downstairs to the kitchen, I made a cup of coffee and took it to the island, then sat on the barstool, sipping the hot black brew.

I let the silence of the house envelope me and ease some of the tension I'd felt these past months. It was good to have someone else here helping me care for Peter. I'd been doing it alone for so long now that I hadn't realized until this morning when I'd opened the door to Hope just how hard it had been.

Hope.

She was a breath of fresh air. I felt lighter than I had in months. Her presence was a beacon of hope. I prayed my little nephew felt something good because of her being here.

My phone buzzed in my back pocket, so I pulled it out and glanced at the screen. My chest tightened as if a thousand-pound elephant had just sat on it.

"Hello, Mother."

"Darius, hello. How are you and Peter doing?"

"Never been better."

"I seriously doubt that, which is why I'm calling. Listen, your father and I are free this weekend. We'd like to see you and Peter. Please come to the house for lunch on Sunday."

I bit back the vehement rejection on the tip of my tongue. Right now, with everything that I was dealing with, I didn't want to fight with my mother. It would not hurt to let her have a few hours with Peter. I doubted my father would even be there on Sunday. And it would be good for Peter to get out of the house for a bit. I made a mental note to talk to Hope about some planned outings for Peter.

"Is that a yes?"

"Of course, Mother. We'll see you at twelve."

"Good. Say hello to Peter for me."

"Sure."

She hung up, leaving me holding a dead phone to my ear. I breathed through the flare of irritation I felt because of our conversation and then put my cell in my back pocket. The light sound of footsteps on the wooden floor had me turning just as Hope and Peter appeared in the doorway together.

"Hey, Bud." I walked over to him and swung him up into my arms, enjoying the feel of him against my chest. He wrapped his arms around my neck.

"Guess what, Uncle Dar! Ms. Martinez is going to stay with me today."

"And how do you feel about that?" I asked, hoping he loved it as much as I thought he did.

"Great!" He fist-pumped the air. It was the most excited I'd seen him in three months.

I met Hope's gaze and saw her answering smile curve her lips. The last of the tension between my shoulders slipped away. I'd made the right decision by asking her for help.

"Thank you."

"No worries!"

I nodded. She didn't know it yet, but she'd just gained my loyalty for life. Anything she needed, she just had to ask me and I would make it happen. She'd been here less than an hour, and already Peter was smiling and fist-pumping the air in victory. I would be eternally grateful to her.

"All right! How about some breakfast, huh? What do you say? Want some eggs and toast?"

Peter squirmed in my arms, wanting to get down. I set him down and watched as he ran off into the living room. He pulled out the small bag of Legos I kept in an Ottoman and began putting the pieces together.

"I guess breakfast is still a no."

"Don't worry, I'll take care of it. I'm sure there's something I can get him to eat. If I remember correctly, he loved pepperoni pizza."

"Pizza for breakfast?" I rubbed the achy spot at the nape of my neck.

"The cure for any starving four-year-old." She smiled.

"Right. Why not?"

Pizza wasn't the conventional way to go at nine in the morning, but, well, if it got Peter to eat, who was I to object?

"Is there anything I need to know before you head out the door?"

"My cell phone number?" I asked.

"Right." With a laugh, she pulled her phone out of her jeans pocket just as the screen lit up with an incoming call before going blank. The laughter died on her lips and in her eyes.

"Everything okay?"

"Never been better." She spoke the same lie I'd told my mother just minutes ago.

"I seriously doubt that."

She lifted her gaze, meeting mine head-on. "It's nothing." She shook her head and smiled, attempting to reassure me, but her smile lacked the joy it had moments ago.

I remembered how her phone had gone off yesterday. I closed the distance between us, then lowering my voice, I asked, "Are you in trouble?"

"No! It's nothing like that."

White heat flared in the pit of my stomach and sent blood rushing to the surface of my skin. I cupped her elbow, stepping closer to her. "Your boyfriend?"

Her cheeks turned pink. "No. Not anymore."

That strangling feeling eased just enough so I could breathe again. "Good."

The color in her cheeks deepened. She caught her bottom lip between her teeth. I saw the heat in her eyes before she looked away. Moments later, she was taking a step back so that my hand fell from her. Her retreat knocked some sense into me. I glanced at Peter, but he was still sitting on the living room floor, playing with his Lego set.

I gave her my cell phone number and programmed hers into my phone as well.

"Also, you should know, I have a landline in the livingroom."

"A what now?"

"A landline." I frowned at her. "You know, it's a phone connected to the house." I stopped when I saw the wicked grin spreading across her face.

"I know what a landline is. Though, other than my mom and dad, you're the only other person I've met who has one."

"I had it put in when Pete came to live with me. My phone number's taped next to it, in case he ever wants to call me when I'm not with him. It hardly ever rings, though."

"Got it." She smiled up at me, shoving her phone into her back jeans pocket.

I pulled my wallet out and handed her my Centurion card. Her eyes went wide at the sight of the black Amex card.

"Is that what I think it is?"

I shrugged, but the smug pleasure made me smile. I doubted her ex-boyfriend had one of those.

"I thought these were a myth."

"Hang on to it for a while."

"Darius." She laughed, shaking her head as she held the card out for me to take it back. "It's pizza from down the street, not Paris. I got it."

Now I was the one feeling flushed. And stupid. She was right. I was being a jerk. Damn if I hadn't wanted to impress the hell out of her, though. Seriously, what in the world was wrong with me? I wasn't the type to flaunt my wealth. Hell, I hated it when a woman wanted me for my money. Why was I showing Hope my bottom line?

I ignored her outstretched hand and the credit card in it. Turning, I headed into the living room instead.

"Hey, Bud." I couched down next to Peter. When he looked up, I dropped a kiss on my brother's forehead, and saw the answering smile on Alice's mouth. He was beautiful, and the pain that my brother and his wife were missing this twisted my heart.

"Have fun with Ms. Martinez, okay? I'll be back soon, but you can call me if you need me."

"Okay."

I ignored Peter's solemn response, knowing it was only because he hated goodbyes. It was difficult walking away from him. But his therapist was right. I needed to get back to work, and Peter had his whole life ahead of him to live. We needed to get him past the seclusion I'd inadvertently imposed on the two of us. I'd brought him home with me and closed the doors to the world outside. We'd developed a routine together; the two of us alone here in this house. Now it was time for us to let the outside world in.

I turned and found Hope standing close by with the black credit card still in her hand.

"I'll be back by five. Is that okay?"

"Yes, of course. Don't worry about us. I've got him."

Her quiet reassurance had me releasing the pent-up breath I'd been holding. Peter was comfortable with her, and she was like sunshine coming in after the storm. Everything was going to be okay. Finally, after three months, it felt like both Peter and I were going to be all right.

CHAPTER 5

HOPE

It was eight-fifteen by the time I pulled into a vacant parking spot in front of my apartment building. Shutting off my car, I sat in the darkness for a moment, gathering my thoughts. I'd spent the day with Peter, putting Lego pieces together, reading to him and watching his favorite shows. Darius had come home closer to six than five and then had insisted that I stay for dinner. I hadn't left their house until a little after seven-thirty to make the forty-five-minute drive to my apartment. Yes, it was late, and I was exhausted, but I felt like I was on cloud nine! And I got to do it again tomorrow.

I was smiling as I got out of my car, locking it behind me. I fished for my apartment key in my small handbag.

"Where have you been?"

I yelped. Whirling around, my heart rate spiking painfully, I gasped.

"Jesus Christ, Johnathan! What in the world? What are you doing here?"

Johnathan was standing behind me. I looked around, but we were the only two on the landing. I exhaled the rush of panic that had assaulted me at the unexpected sound of a man's voice behind me. The last time I'd seen him had been the night of our dinner, when we broke up. He seemed taller than I remembered him, but he looked like he'd lost some weight. His normally muscular frame looked slimmer and much more toned. All the same, he loomed over me.

"I've been calling you. Where are you coming from this late at night?"

Why was he standing on my landing? I hadn't seen him when I approached my door, so either he'd been lurking in the shadows, or he'd followed me up the stairs.

I ignored the chill tingling up my spine and resumed looking for my keys in my handbag. I didn't answer him until I had them in my hand.

"Work. I've taken a winter break job."

The angry expression on his face softened slightly. Now he just looked his usual irritated self. "I've been calling you."

"I heard you the first time."

"So, is your phone broken or something?" he demanded.

"There's nothing wrong with my phone. We broke up three months ago. Why are you calling me?"

He grabbed my arm unexpectedly, stepping closer to me, and sparking my irritation at his hold. I had to crane my neck to maintain eye contact. The unease of the situation had another shiver running down my spine. Johnathan was usually even-keeled, even detached from his emotions. While I hadn't seen or communicated with him in a while, and he could have changed, his behavior still struck me as 'off'.

"I miss you," he spoke softly, confidently, as if I hadn't just reminded him we were no longer together.

"Can I come in? Can we talk?"

"We have nothing to talk about, Johnathan. It's late. I'm not even sure what you're doing here."

"I needed to see you. I needed to talk to you and you aren't answering my calls."

"So, you came to my apartment, and what? You laid in wait when you realized I wasn't home?"

Johnathan released my arm. He ran a hand through his blond hair before pressing his palm flat against the doorjamb next to me. I could feel the frustration coming off him in waves. My insides quivered, and a tightness squeezed my chest. I suddenly felt too hot standing there in my coat.

"It wasn't like that. Look." He sighed as he reached for me. "I miss you."

He wrapped me up in his muscular arms and pressed my head against his chest before I fully comprehended his intent to hug me. I pressed my hands against his chest and pushed, but he barely budged. His fingers pressed against the back of my head, caressing my scalp. A flutter of pleasure settled in my stomach at his touch. It felt good resting against his chest. It felt good just being held.

Maybe it was because it had been months since I'd had any physical contact with anyone, not counting the random hugs from the kids in my class. I was human, and it felt good to connect with another human being.

An image of Darius holding my hand and walking me toward Peter rose unexpectedly in my mind. I pulled away from Johnathan and pushed against him, hard, breaking free of his touch.

"Hope, I've been miserable without you. I was sick for close to a month, and I realized as I was lying in bed in pain, every part of my body aching, unable to smell anything, taste anything, that all I wanted was you. I missed your smile, your gentleness. How good we were together."

"You were sick?"

He nodded. "And all I wanted was you."

"Not your work? Or Janice?"

He had the good sense to look away, but only for a second. His gaze was steady when he met my eyes again. "I was wrong to let those things come between us. I wouldn't make the same mistake twice."

God, he was so tempting. It was tempting to believe that he would not put me on the back burner when his work began demanding his time. It was tempting to believe I would come first, but the reality was different. His illness had been his wake-up call, and he probably realized that he wanted a companion in his life. Someone who would take care of him, love him. I wanted someone who would do that for me, too, but the two of us together just didn't fit. He wasn't the one for me, just as I wasn't the woman for him.

"I didn't know you were sick. I'm glad you're better, Johnathan, but the reasons we broke up remain the same. Our break-up was for the best."

I put the key in the lock and turned it. He stopped me, his hand on the door.

"Give me a second chance."

"I can't."

"Why not?" His jaw clenched, his face hardening. "Is there someone else?"

Darius's smiling face flashed through my mind. I shook my head to clear thoughts of him and focused on Johnathan. "There's no one else. I just don't want to go down the lonely road of being in a relationship with you."

"I've changed, Hope. I promise you. You know what? I'm going to show you I've changed. I'm going to win you back."

"Please, don't. I just want you to respect my decision, okay? Just please leave me alone."

I slipped through the open door and closed it behind me.

Walking into my kitchen, I opened the refrigerator and grabbed the bottle of white wine I kept chilling on the door, poured myself a drink in a short tumbler, and swallowed most of it in one go.

What was I doing? Just two days ago, I'd been complaining about being lonely. Had being in a relationship with Johnathan been so bad? He was here offering to give me the relationship I wanted and I was turning him down. Why? For what? I didn't want to be a fool and end up lonely. I wanted marriage, kids, love.

Love.

There it was.

I didn't love Johnathan. The basic foundation of any good relationship was missing. I could date him again, but I would only draw out the inevitable. I'd made the right decision by walking away that night. Johnathan and I weren't in love with each other. I wasn't sure we ever had been.

Good bones.

It was what I wanted. A relationship that was built on a good foundation - love, friendship, desire, and mutual respect. And passion. Lots and lots of passion. Johnathan and I didn't have that together.

Darius's sensual mouth crossed my mind. I felt a million butterflies take flight in my stomach. Something existed with Darius that I hadn't experienced with Johnathan. It was enough to reassure me that I'd made the right decision not giving into Johnathan.

"Good bones," I whispered in my silent apartment.

It was what I deserved, and I was going to wait for it.

CHAPTER 6

DARIUS

I opened the door seconds after Hope rang the doorbell. Peter barreled past me and wrapped his arms around her legs. We'd both been waiting for her.

"Hi!" Her musical laughter filled my foyer, wrapping around me like a warm blanket. Apricots. That's it. She smelled like apricots and fresh flowers. Absolutely delicious.

"How are you?" I studied her smiling face. My heart felt too big in my chest. She looked tired and there were shadows under her eyes.

"I'm great!" She smiled, but it didn't reach her eyes.

"No offense, Hope, but you look exhausted. Did you sleep okay last night?"

"I'm fine."

I shut the door behind her and helped her remove her full-length winter coat, hanging it up in the entryway closet. With a hand on her back, I led her and Peter toward the kitchen. She helped Peter onto one of the bar stools at the island before sitting in the chair next to him.

I placed Peter's plate of scrambled eggs, bacon, and toast in front of him and didn't miss the way he scrunched up his nose. The sadness that was never far away settled on his face.

Great! Another breakfast bites the dust.

I turned back to face the kitchen sink, bracing my hands against it. *Shawn, help me. I'm dying here.*

Taking a deep breath, I faced Hope. "This isn't too much for you, is it?"

I couldn't get enough oxygen. Inhaling deeply, I tried to calm my panic. What if she said yes? What if she couldn't watch Peter anymore? Had I opened my little boy up to more pain?

"Of course not! I'm fine. Don't you need to get going?"

Despite her denial, I still had a sour taste in my mouth. I took another deep breath, hoping to quench the sudden overwhelming feeling of dread. I needed this woman standing in front of me. Peter and I both did.

"Hope, promise me you'll talk to me if there's a problem."

She nodded. "Everything's fine, Darius. Please don't worry. And please don't be late because of me."

I hesitated, unwilling to leave the two of them alone. She was right, though. I needed a haircut before I got into the office. Brian, Hayden, and I were meeting for the groundbreaking, and I still had to revise a couple of the designs for Project Resilience. Bottom line, I had a ton of work to do and I needed to get moving.

"Yeah, you're right." I pulled out my black Amex card again and ignored her laugher as I handed it to her. "Just in case."

"Right. Just in case Peter and I want to have lunch in New York today."

I enjoyed her teasing me. It had been a while since anyone

had done that. In fact, come to think about it, the last person to tease me had been Shawn.

"You like New York?"

She frowned, then shrugged her shoulders. Her smile dimmed, and she looked unsure, shy almost.

"Who doesn't?" she asked.

"Yeah, me too."

Before Shawn's death, when life was still carefree, I wouldn't have missed the opportunity to invite a beautiful woman to New York for the weekend. I would have whisked her away in first class to Manhattan. Or, better yet, I would have asked Rafe, my buddy, to borrow his private jet. Anything to impress my girl.

I looked down at my nephew sitting between us. He'd eaten all his bacon and was now nibbling on his toast. The eggs sat untouched on his plate. Yeah, that life was over. I was treading water and barely keeping my head above the surface. Messing around with Hope was out of the question.

"I'll be back by five."

"See you then."

I kissed Pete on the top of his silky hair before leaving the two of them in the kitchen together. Moments later, I was backing my F150 out of my garage and heading down the driveway, counting the minutes until five.

CHAPTER 7

HOPE

"So, Pete, sweetie, tell me, what's wrong with Uncle Dar's eggs?"

I ate a spoonful of said eggs and sighed at the cheesy flavor. The scrambled eggs were delicious. But they weren't Pete's favorite.

He looked at the eggs, then at me with wet eyes. His head fell, hanging low on his shoulders.

"They're not the way Mommy made them."

"Ah, I see." So, my hunch was correct. Pete did like eggs, just not scrambled eggs. "Can you tell me how your mommy made them?"

Pete looked down at his plate full of eggs. He shook his head. His sadness was back, like a blanket covering him.

"It's okay, sweetie. We'll figure it out."

Darius must not know either, or he would have been making Pete's eggs that way to begin with. Pete didn't like scrambled eggs. The question was, how had Alice made his eggs? Hm, there were only so many ways you could do eggs for breakfast, and for a four-year-old.

I pulled out the tray of eggs from the refrigerator. I'd seen the look of abject failure on Darius's face yesterday, and today when he realized once again Pete wasn't eating his breakfast. Pete's disappointment at the sight of the scrambled eggs on his plate had also been hard to miss. We were going to fix this today.

It was a minor thing, and it was something I could focus on instead of Johnathan and the constant questions about whether I was making a mistake by turning him down.

Thoughts of my relationship with Johnathan had consumed me last night. I'd tossed and turned, remembering how he'd looked, how he'd felt, and wondering if I shouldn't give him another chance. We were good together; I supposed.

Yeah, like acne on a fourteen-year-old.

Who was I kidding? We worked but only because I had been willing to take a back seat to Johnathan's needs. I'd fallen in line and allowed him to run the show. He'd decided when we went out, where we went, and what topics we chatted about during our fancy dinners. It hadn't worked for me. I'd ended up bored out of my mind in our relationship and lonely most of the time.

You're lonely now.

Yes, I was, but at least I was lonely alone. And it felt better being alone and lonely than being lonely in a committed relationship that wasn't going anywhere.

Good bones! I still wanted it. Johnathan and I hadn't had it and I doubt that anything had changed in the last three months.

Helping Darius care for Peter was helping me. So, what if I was experiencing a few heart palpitations at the sight of my employer? That wasn't altogether too bad, was it? Darius was handsome and witty. He was easy on the eye, and I enjoyed bantering back and forth with him.

His consideration this morning had taken me by surprise, however. He was a very discerning man. I'd grown used to being ignored in my relationship with Johnathan, and in the months following our break-up. There hadn't been anyone who'd concerned themselves with my well-being. Darius's attention this morning had made me uncomfortable, but only because it felt a lot like good bones.

Minutes later, I placed a sliced, hard-boiled egg on a saucer in front of Pete. He looked at it, met my eyes, and shook his head. I watched as he ran off to the living room to play with his Lego pieces. Okay, hard-boiled eggs weren't it either. Back to the drawing board.

Ten minutes later, I called him over. I set a new saucer in front of him as he climbed onto the stool.

"Poached?" I asked, hoping I'd hit the jackpot.

"Nope!" Pete climbed off the stool and ran off.

"Okay, then."

I set the saucer aside and reached for a fresh egg. Not boiled or poached. Not scrambled. An omelet maybe? Now things were getting complicated. What would Alice have put in Pete's omelet? Choices for an omelet were endless. I opened the refrigerator. Or maybe not so, I thought, as I studied the meager contents of Darius's fridge. Looked like Peter and I were going grocery shopping today with Darius's black American Express card. I chuckled as I pulled out the three remaining stalks of green onions, the almost empty packet of shredded cheese, and a wrinkled-looking red bell pepper. On second thought, I put the bell pepper back and grabbed a tomato instead. Best to keep it simple in case I didn't get the contents of the omelet correct.

"Pete, come here, Bud!"

He came over, an expression of excitement on his face. I

waited until he sat before placing the omelet in front of him. I watched him as he watched the omelet. He said nothing for a moment and I was thinking I might have hit the jackpot when he sighed. It was a very sad sigh of defeat. He shook his head, picked up his fork, and took a bite. I held my breath. His head popped up. He met my eyes. I waited; my breath caught in my throat. He smiled and took another bite.

"Is this it?" I asked with a smile. He was such a handsome little boy, and when he smiled, he was a heart-stealer.

"Nope!" He took another bite of the omelet before setting his fork down and dashing off.

So, it wasn't an omelet, but he didn't mind eating an omelet. That was good to know. We'd switch to omelets instead of scrambled eggs in the meantime, but I wasn't giving up. I pulled my phone out of my pocket and googled different ways to cook eggs.

"Huh." I'd tried most of the suggestions on the list except that one. Could it be…? I searched through the cupboards until I found Darius's frying pan and a bottle of olive oil.

Soon the kitchen smelled like fried eggs. I was just plating the finished egg when Pete came into the kitchen and climbed onto the stool. His eyes were shiny, his little bottom lip trembling. I set it down in front of him. He reached for his fork, broke the piece off, and took a bite of the fried egg.

Tears filled my eyes as I watched him eat the entire fried egg. I was laughing out loud by the time he'd cleaned his plate. He got off the stool and ran around the counter to hug me. I picked him up, squeezing him tight. We were both laughing, tears flowing down our faces.

"What's going on?"

I turned, Pete still in my arms. Darius was standing just inside the kitchen. He'd come in from the hallway leading to the garage. He looked around the counter, his eyes going wide at the sight of all the saucers with differently cooked eggs.

"Uncle Dar!" Pete struggled to get down, and I released my hold on him.

He ran over to Darius, throwing himself at him. Darius picked him up in an easy hug and adjusted him on his hip. My stomach fluttered at the sight of them. I turned away, reaching for a paper towel, and dabbed at my wet cheeks.

"Peter prefers his eggs fried." I turned to face Darius again.

"Really?" Darius looked at Pete, who nodded his head.

Peter placed his hands on his uncle's cheeks and pulled his face down toward him for a quick kiss. Then he wiggled, wanting to get down. When Darius set him down, he ran off to the living room.

"It's the way his mom made them."

"You figured it out." Darius walked toward me.

"Yes." I held his stare, even though doing so made me weak in the knees. That tingling, nervous feeling was back in the pit of my stomach. I wanted to glance away from his glassy greenish-brown eyes, but I couldn't break eye contact to save my life. I pressed both my hands against the countertop and leaned in for its support.

"What are you doing back so soon?"

"I forgot some documents I'm presenting to my partners this afternoon."

"Oh."

"Now I'm glad I did. I get to share this victory with you."

His hand settled over mine on the counter. "Thank you."

My stomach somersaulted in response to the intense look of gratitude in his eyes. I tried to speak but was at a loss for words, thanks to that look. Darius was genuinely good looking. His steady eye contact left me holding my breath. My face felt hot and flushed. I wondered why he was single.

Wait, why did I think he was single? Chances are, Darius had a girlfriend, or someone he was interested in. He'd been busy the past three months grieving and taking care of Pete. He was back at work now, and perhaps he would also resume his dating?

"Yeah, of course." His fingers caressed my hand. I looked down at them, clearing my throat. "Actually, I'm glad you're here. You're saving me a phone call to you. Do you mind if I took Pete to the grocery store? Your fridge is just a tad bit bare."

"Sure. I don't mind. There's a market down the main street, still here inside the community."

"I'll find it."

"So…" He lifted his hand, and I felt the loss of his touch. He rubbed the nape of his neck. "Does this mean you plan on cooking dinner?"

"It does. Do you have any special requests?"

He smiled. "Lucky for us, Pete's not so picky about dinner."

"What about you?" My heart still beat a mile a minute. My mouth was dry. I swallowed, licked my lips, and met his eyes. Seriously, he had the nicest hazel eyes I'd seen in a long time.

"Lasagna would be nice. But you don't have to make one. There's an Italian restaurant next to the supermarket. You can just order one to go."

I could do that, or I could make it from scratch. My mom made a mean lasagna, and she'd taught me how to cook. I could handle his favorite dish.

"No worries!"

"Okay." He glanced in the garage's direction. I could sense his hesitation to go, despite him running late.

"I know you've got a busy day, so I'll let you go."

He smiled, nodded, and moved away from the counter. He was almost out the door when he stopped and turned.

"I'm glad you're here, Hope." His eyes were soft and bright.

"Me too."

Moments later, he was gone, and I was alone in the kitchen with my racing heart, wondering what in the world was this attraction that I was feeling for Darius. It had come out of nowhere. But, as I remembered the way he had had looked at me a moment ago, I wondered if he was feeling the same thing.

CHAPTER 8

DARIUS

I glanced at the time on the bottom of my computer screen and wondered how in the world it wasn't much, much later than the last time I'd checked. I wanted it to be five o'clock with me sitting in my dining room eating Hope's lasagna, watching her smile as I devoured it.

"It's good to have you back," Brian said.

I looked up as my two business partners walked through my open doorway. Brian was tall, blond, and muscular. He had his shirt sleeves rolled up his arms already, despite it still being work hours. He clearly hadn't been missing his gym sessions.

"From the looks of that smile on his face, he's happy to be back too," Hayden retorted.

Hayden was the opposite of Brian. He was wearing a navy-blue suit, a white shirt, and a blue tie. Tall, with dark hair, and a lean, well-toned body, he was always well put together. Not a wrinkle in sight.

Both men had grins on their faces. Hayden picked up the baseball on my desk and twirled it around his fingers. I could hear Shawn's whoop of joy and feel his slap on my back when I'd caught it.

I cleared my throat, breathing through the tightness in my chest, and did my best to smile.

"I wouldn't lie; it feels great to be back in the office with you guys."

I had missed the hustle and bustle of the company while I'd been away caring for Peter. Even though I'd handled a few minor details from my home office, it hadn't compared to being back in the thick of things. Listening to the distant hum of chatter outside my office as our staff carried out their duties made me feel as though I was an intricate part of the wheel that turned Gemini Inc.

I'd needed the time to heal. Work was the last thing I'd been able to handle after Shawn's death. Pete had needed me at home with him. So, even though we'd successfully acquired the land for Project Resilience and had launched headfirst into preparations for the next phase, the business had taken a back seat for me as I'd focused on Pete. Brian and Hayden had done an excellent job coping with two absent partners. Luckily, they'd been able to do both Shawn's and my jobs, and the company had continued to advance rather than flounder.

"I can't thank you guys enough for the way you both stepped up."

"Don't mention it," Hayden said.

"How's Peter handling you being back to work?"

I met Brian's sharp eyes. "Better than I thought he would, actually."

"Really?"

"Yeah." I smiled. "I think it has something to do with his new nanny."

"His nanny?"

"Do you remember Hope Martinez, his teacher?"

"The woman at the funeral?"

"The pretty brunette?"

Brian and Hayden both spoke at the same time. Hayden threw the baseball into the air and caught it before tossing it up again.

My stomach hardened at Hayden's description, and my back turned rigid. "You think she's pretty?"

Hayden caught the ball and turned to face me with a look of confusion on his face. "Yeah, she's pretty. I've seen prettier, but…" His confusion gave way to shock and his eyes widened as his mouth formed a perfect O.

"Wait a minute!" He was suddenly in front of me, leaning over my desk. "Do *you* think she's pretty?"

I snorted and pushed my chair back, eager to get away from his heated stare. Hayden was intense when he was hunting for answers. He was one of my best friends and my business partner. I usually enjoyed watching him ferret insider information out of our competitors, but Hope wasn't a topic I wanted to discuss with him.

"She's Peter's nanny."

"Answer the question."

"I'm not answering your question."

"Ah-ha! You do think she's pretty."

"She works for me. And even if she didn't, I would still tread carefully."

"Why's that?" Brian asked.

I met his curious stare. "Because she's a friend."

I remembered how she'd stood with me during one of my darkest moments, offering me silent support and comfort as I'd grieved at Shawn and Alice's gravesite. The somber tension in the office told me the other two men remembered that moment, too.

"Yeah, friends are rare." Hayden finally broke the silence. He tossed the ball in the air again and caught it.

"And you should see her with Peter. She's awesome."

I smiled as I remembered how she had solved the egg situation. Shawn and I had both grown up with nannies. They'd been people paid to meet all our physical needs, with no thought to our emotional needs. We were a job to them. They hadn't been paid to love us, or even to form any kind of attachment to us.

Hope had done more than just make sure Pete had his breakfast. She'd taken the time to discover why the scrambled eggs made him so sad. In the process, she'd brought a bit of his mom back into his life. Pete was happy, thanks to her. In making him happy, she'd relieved a sore point for me.

There was no way I was going to risk my nephew's happiness by sleeping with Hope.

"So, the nanny's off-limits." Hayden smiled. "For you anyway."

"For everyone." The thought of Hayden putting the moves on Hope had acid churning in my stomach.

"Hey, man." I looked up to find Brian standing in front of me. "All joking aside, you're doing a great job with Pete. I'm proud of you."

The churning in my stomach eased. I stretched my hand out, and taking hold of Brian's outstretched hand, I allowed him to pull me in for a quick embrace.

I'd never wanted children, but fate had given me Peter. My desire to accomplish more drove me. It meant Gemini Inc. always came first. We all put the business first.

Then Shawn had died, and overnight, I'd become the sole guardian of my nephew. Not a second went by that I didn't fear I was making the same mistakes my parents had made with me. Then, there was also the constant worry that I couldn't give Peter everything he needed.

Thank God for Hope.

I don't know how it had happened so quickly, but she'd made a difference in my life. I couldn't blow it with her.

"Thank you, Brian. I appreciate you saying that."

"Anyway, look, man. There's something we need to discuss with you," Hayden started somberly.

"What is it?"

"Allen's coming to town the week after Christmas. He wants to meet with us."

Brian, Hayden, and I had made the decision to approach Allen Kent's investment company for additional financing for Project Resilience shortly after Shawn's death. It had made sense not to be stretched so thin when we were trying to navigate waters without Shawn. As far as I knew, Kent was coming through with an investment and we were scheduled to break ground on the project in early January. "Okay."

Brian sat in the chair in front of my desk. "There's a little more to it than that. I've heard through the grapevine that he now has reservations about doing business with us. He believes we are 'playboy billionaires'," Brian announced dryly, making air quotes, "and he's hesitant to commit all in with three guys he thinks are hugely unstable. Shawn was a large part of the draw for him to undertake this project with us. He trusted and respected him, and following his death, he wanted to help. Now, months later, he's looking at us personally and having second thoughts."

"He knows we're good for the financing," I said.

"He'd feel better if we had another investor."

"Who's he proposing?"

"Rafe."

I snorted. "Rafael Bodine has bigger fish to fry. He's not going to invest in our project."

I knew Rafe well enough to be confident of that. He'd gone to college with Shawn, Hayden, and Brian. While the three guys had asked me to team up with them and we'd started our real estate development company, Rafe had gone out on his own, forming Phoenix, his construction company. We were all friends, and Brian and Hayden were even in the same men's breakfast group with Rafe, but Rafe was as cutthroat in business as they came. He wasn't the type of man to partner with anyone on anything, unless he planned to cut them out himself and keep the gains.

Coming in on our project wasn't going to appeal to Rafe. Perhaps Allen had suggested Rafe Bodine because he intended to pull out. That would be a costly setback for us, considering that we had so much of our liquid cash tied up in the success of this project. Any unprecedented delays could set us back.

"Where do you think I heard it from? Rafe called me to give me a heads-up. He said our deal with Kent wasn't as solid as we thought, since Kent was floating the idea of Rafe investing in the project with him.

"Allen Kent can go screw himself." Hayden scoffed.

"True, but he's likely to take his money with him. Do we know exactly what his sudden objection is?" I asked Brian.

"It's our first major construction project. We're all young, single, unattached. Nothing to hold our feet to the fire. No one to hold us accountable."

"All crap!" Hayden snorted in disgust.

I agreed with Hayden, but I said nothing. Other investors and business acquaintances had said the same thing as they walked away from a deal with us, concerned that Gemini Inc. was too young, too untethered for the responsibilities of the projects we were trying to land. Things had gradually improved with the success of each new project. Our business had really soared after Shawn married Alice. It had been easy to have Shawn be the face for Gemini Inc., while Brian, Hayden, and I remained the confirmed bachelors in the background. We'd even made fun of the setup, completely aware that we were putting the bulk of the responsibility for the image of the company on Shawn. Now that he was gone, business partners like Kent believed the stability of the company had passed with him. How did we go about repairing that?

"Brian, can we set up a face-to-face meeting with Allen? See if we can iron out his concerns?"

Brian nodded. "I'm sure I can arrange something. Were you thinking after Christmas?"

"Yes, since it may be difficult to do it before. Definitely before the new year starts. We need to put this to rest well before the ground-breaking ceremony in January."

"All right. Let me see what I can arrange."

"Now that's out of the way, can we get down to business?" Hayden said, pulling out a chair at my meeting desk and sitting down. "Have you looked at the projections for the ground-breaking? I emailed it to you this afternoon. Care to go over it?"

I glanced at the clock and felt a moment of indecision. It was four-fifteen, and if I started this with Hayden, there was no way we would finish in time for me to make it home to Peter and Hope for dinner at five. Hayden was already pulling up the spreadsheets on his iPad, though. He fully expected my butt in a chair at that desk.

Just like that, here I was, torn between work and home. How the hell had Shawn balanced the two so well? I didn't know. I just knew there was no way to be in two places at once and someone or something was always going to suffer because of it. Today, it could not be Gemini Inc.

CHAPTER 9

HOPE

"I'm sorry!" Darius's voice greeted me through the phone line. "I'm just leaving the office. I'm afraid I wouldn't make it in time to eat with you guys."

The kitchen clock said it was already quarter to five. Peter sat at the table coloring quietly, while we waited for Darius to arrive.

"Okay, no worries." I smiled, despite my disappointment, hoping to take away some of the pressure I heard in his voice. "It's no problem. I'll see you when you get here."

We hung up, and I turned to face Peter.

"All right, Pete, sweetie, time to eat. Would you please pack up the coloring books and crayons?"

"Okay."

I cut into the hot lasagna and fixed two plates. Walking over to the kitchen table, I placed one of the plates in front of Peter and took a seat next to him. Satisfaction made me smile as he dug his fork into the pie.

"Careful, it's hot."

He blew on the forkful before biting into it.

He made a humming noise.

"You like it?" I laughed.

"Yummy," he said, digging his fork into the pie for more.

We ate with enthusiasm, and in and between mouthfuls, kept up a comfortable banter about his favorite TV show and the books he wanted me to read to him tonight. When we were finished eating, we deposited our plates into the sink.

"Okay, Bud." I took his hand. "Let's get you a bath and then ready for bed."

"Not yet. I want to wait for Uncle Dar."

"Uncle Dar's on his way home. Let's go get a bath before he comes. Then you'll have more time to spend with him. Maybe he can even join us for story time."

Peter thought about it for a second and then nodded, walking willingly with me to the bathroom.

Turning on the faucet to fill the tub, I added a cupful of his lavender body wash under the flowing water. Soon, the relaxing scent filled the air as bubbles floated on the surface of the water. I threw in a few of his toy boats and a couple rubber duckies for good measure before turning to Peter and helping him undress.

We were almost through with the bath when Peter slapped one of his toy boats across the surface, pushing water over the edge and splashing me in the process. I gasped, caught between surprised laughter and a groan of horror as water washed over my torso, soaking my shirt and the front of my jeans.

"Peter!"

We both looked around to see Darius standing there, a horrified expression on his face.

"Uncle Dar!" Peter exclaimed, unaware of the mess he'd

made or that he'd soaked me entirely straight through my shirt.

"It's okay." I pulled my wet shirt away from my chest. Darius moved quickly, grabbing a towel from the linen closet, and closing the space between us to hand it to me.

"Thank you," I murmured, suddenly very self-conscious. I pressed the fluffy towel against my chest.

He looked good despite the long day he'd had. Standing tall above me, dressed in work pants and with the sleeves of his white shirt rolled up to his elbows, he looked every inch the handsome billionaire.

"I'm sorry." Darius squatted next to me. He kept his gaze dead set on my face.

"It's okay, really."

"Why don't I grab you a t-shirt to change into and then I'll finish this up?"

"Okay."

He ruffled Pete's hair before standing up and walking out of the room, taking most of the air with him. I took a deep breath and convinced myself that my nipples were tight and my panties were wet because of the cooling water on my body. It had nothing to do with Peter's hot uncle, and the attractive jolt to my system of finding him there, watching me.

Something about the way his gaze had ghosted over my chest before he'd lifted it, shocked and horrified to meet my eyes, told me that he'd been as taken aback as I had been. The air had crackled with sexual awareness when he'd squatted down next to me. He'd been so close that I could see the darkening of his pupils, the flare of his nostrils with every breath he took and the firm press of his lips that had begged me to press mines to his.

The attraction I felt for Darius had roared front and

center to the forefront of my mind. I'd wanted to lean against him and press my lips against his.

I heard him this time, walking back into the bathroom.

"Here you go."

I took the heather gray sweatshirt he held out to me and stood up, still clutching the towel to my chest. Avoiding his gaze, I walked out of the room and into another bathroom two doors down the hall. A glance in the mirror revealed what I already knew. My cheeks were flushed. My eyes looked dilated. I was aroused. Sexually. And Darius was the object of my desire.

I pressed the towel against my face and groaned in frustration. This was so inappropriate. How the hell had things spiraled so out of control? From day one, there'd been no denying that Darius was a sexually attractive man. But it had always been a back-burner thought. Like dead embers in a fireplace, occasionally glowing, but not alive enough to come to life. But tonight, I was hyperaware of his attractiveness.

My feelings were getting crossed. There was no other explanation for it. I'd been busy in his home, cooking meals, watching Peter, and joking with Darius. It had begun to get twisted in my mind, and suddenly, Darius was looking very attractive to me. But I needed to take a deep breath and go the hell home.

I pulled my wet shirt and bra off, towel-dried, and slipped into his large gray sweatshirt. It was clean and smelled like the laundry detergent he preferred. Thank God for small mercies! I couldn't deal with inhaling Darius's captivating scent all the way home. I needed a break, now, before I did something totally inappropriate that would ruin everything.

I followed the sound of Darius's deep voice and Peter's soft one all the way into Pete's bedroom. Pete sat on the bed, already in his PJs, as Darius dried his hair with a towel. The sight had my stomach dipping and heat flooding through my body. I felt the yearning even as I chastised myself for being a fool.

"Hey, look who's back." Darius glanced over his shoulder at me. "Everything okay?"

"Yes." I smiled, walking over to the other side of the bed and sitting next to Peter. "I'd best be going," I murmured softly.

Darius glanced at his watch, folding up the towel in his lap. "It's late. I'm sorry I've held you up. Are you good to drive?"

"Yes, of course." I laughed. "It's not too late. Don't worry."

He nodded, though his eyes were serious as he locked his gaze on me.

"Is this still okay? You haven't bitten off more than you can chew, have you?"

I met his gaze across the top of Pete's head. I saw the worry and something else in his eyes that had my heart flipping over in my chest. He wasn't only referring to caring for Peter and the long hours. He was talking about the chemistry between us. I knew he felt it too. Did it also worry him and set him on edge? Was his desire also driving him hard like mine was riding me?

"No, not at all. I love watching Peter, and I like being here."

He nodded. His shoulders seemed to detach from his ears, and the worried expression cleared from his eyes. "Okay."

"I'll leave so you can get this little guy down to bed. He's asked for a total of three stories tonight."

Darius slapped his palms against both his cheeks in mock horror, and Peter and I both laughed.

"The lasagna's still in the oven if you wanted some."

"Yes, I'll take care of it. Thank you, Hope."

"You're welcome."

I kissed Pete on the top of his head and slipped off the

bed. I turned at the door, only to find them both watching me. The warm emotion that blossomed in my chest and flowed through my body felt a lot like love. I denied it with a causal smile and wave of my hand before sailing through the door. But I had to pause and lean against the wall, taking a deep breath, before starting down the stairs. Moments later, I had my purse on my shoulder and I was walking out the front door, locking it behind me, aware that something had happened tonight. Something had changed between Darius and me. Almost as if that attraction that had been humming below the surface all this time had broken free. Now that I knew about it, and now that I'd seen glimpses of it in Darius's eyes, I couldn't deny it. I was attracted to him. What's more, I suspected, I could even possibly be falling for him.

CHAPTER 10

DARIUS

The bar was crowded from wall to wall with men and women in various stages of business dress. Most of the men, like me, had loosened their ties after the long day. Women had draped their jackets over the back of their chairs, revealing shiny, flashy, silky tops that looked like lingerie and begged me to touch.

This was a bad idea. I felt it in my gut.

Sitting next to Hayden, at the bar around the corner, after work, sipping on an icy cold beer left me feeling like I'd turned my back on Peter. Of course I hadn't. Hope had agreed to watch him for me while I ran late, but now, being here felt like taking advantage of her.

"Relax." Hayden bumped his shoulder into mine as he lifted the bottle to his lips and took a long pull. "It's just one beer. When was the last time you went out?"

I shrugged. We both knew it was before Shawn and Alice's accident. There hadn't been much time for socializing over the past three months, and I certainly hadn't missed it. Our living room was as social as Peter and I had gotten since the funeral.

Hayden and Brian had stopped over a couple times to have a beer and a game of poker with me after Peter had gone to bed for the night. But causally hanging out at a bar and sipping on a beer felt like it belonged to someone else's life.

"Yeah, you're right. I should probably get going though. I don't want to keep Hope too long."

"Where did you say she lives?"

I hadn't said. The icy, bitter brew soothed my throat on the way down. I lowered my bottle and glanced at Hayden. "Out in Spring."

He whistled slowly. "That's quite a drive from your place. Hell, it takes fifteen minutes just getting out of McKnight Grove. Any place is quite a ways from you."

I chuckled, but he was right. The large master-planned community sat on a huge piece of land, complete with a beautifully developed eighteen-hole golf course and country club. It was luxurious and secluded, offering everything its residents would need or want.

"Does she drive to and from your place every day?"

"Yeah, she does, actually." I frowned at the hassling thoughts that had suddenly flooded my mind, thanks to Hayden's questions. I didn't enjoy watching Hope drive away every day, especially on the evenings that I worked late. She usually arrived at the house as early as seven, which meant she'd been on the road at least since six-fifteen if she was to make it to my home with traffic by that time. She was leaving home early and getting home late. What if she decided the schedule was too much and she couldn't keep watching Pete?

I should head home. What was I thinking coming out for drinks with Hayden? It was a selfish thing to do. I should be rushing home so Hope could head out early. Only, I didn't want her to leave.

"She should move into your guest room."

"What?" I snapped at Hayden.

He looked at me and must have seen the shocked expression on my face because he shrugged before taking another long drink from his bottle of beer.

"Makes sense for her to just stay at your place, don't you think? It would save her the time and hassle of traveling back and forth. At least during the week. You should have told her the job was live-in."

It did make sense. But the thought of Hope in the house with me and Peter had me shifting uncomfortably in my chair. Hope was funny and smart. We were cool. But she was also beautiful. There was an underlying tension that hummed under the surface of all our interactions. Chemistry, I suppose, was what it was called? It had been a while since I'd experienced it, but I wasn't too far gone that I didn't realize it was the type of attraction that typically led to a woman and me falling into my bed. Hope and I had chemistry. It was just right there on the tip of my tongue, or the end of her smile that lasted a beat too long. Or a glance that lingered.

"I don't know."

Hayden stared at me; his bottle forgotten on the bar in front of him.

"It makes sense. What's not to know?"

I stared straight ahead, my hands wrapped around my beer bottle. How could I explain to Hayden that I was attracted to my nanny? He would make a big deal about it. More importantly, I kept my mouth shut because I didn't want to talk about Hope with Hayden, or Brian, or any other man for that matter. This thing between us was new and sweet like her fruity perfume. It was mine, separate from the reality and demands of my life. I didn't want to share it with anyone.

Yeah, her sleeping under my roof was probably definitely not a good idea.

"It might send the wrong message to Peter."

"Peter's four. What's he going to think? She's already watching him all day. And I suspect she's putting him to bed some nights too. Hey, we both know I don't know a thing about kids, right? But, it just makes sense for the poor woman not to have that commute every day."

"You think I should ask her to move in?"

"Yeah, why not? You've got the space."

I drained my bottle and set it aside. Hayden ordered another one, but I declined. It wasn't about the space. I caught Hayden watching me out of the corner of his eye. The bastard knew it too.

I laughed. "Dude, what are you trying to do?"

"Isn't it obvious?"

"You're insane. Hope's a friend."

"I've got nothing against friends with benefits."

"She's Peter's teacher and she's watching him for me so I can get out to work and help us with this very important project, remember? It's too close to home. I could never risk messing this up."

"What's to mess up? You're single; she's single."

"It's not that simple."

Hayden looked over my shoulder and kept staring. I turned to see the two blonde women sitting at a high-top table not too far from us. They both smiled when they saw us staring. I turned around, feeling the uneasiness take root.

"Right, I'm out of here."

"What? Come on."

"I appreciate it, buddy. But hooking up with a random is the last thing I'm wanting to do now."

"Because you're *wanting* to hook up with Hope."

"Hardly." I snorted, getting to my feet. I pulled my wallet out and dropped two twenty-dollar bills on the table next to my drink.

"Good luck, my friend." I slapped him on the back and walked off.

I was at the door when I finally gave in to the urge and turned around to see Hayden looking at home, standing at the table with the two women.

They were gorgeous and their invitation was clear, but I wasn't in the mood to hook up with a stranger tonight. I wanted to be home with Peter…and Hope. That held far more appeal for me. It was still too soon to figure out why that was.

We were friends.

We got along.

She'd done something wonderful for Peter, giving him back a little bit of his mom. I hadn't lied to Hayden. Hope was too close to home. I couldn't risk an affair with her that'd ruin this arrangement we had.

Gemini was important to me, just as it had been to Shawn. Right now, it was Pete I cared most about. His well-being mattered to me above all else. I'd promised myself I would put him first, and so I had to think about what would be best for him. Sleeping with Hope would only complicate things unnecessarily. It was the definition of a bad decision, and I wasn't going to get caught making one of those. Not when Peter was likely to pay the price for my indiscretion.

CHAPTER 11

HOPE

A week into our arrangement, Darius, Peter, and I had settled into a comfortable routine. I arrived early every morning just a little before Darius departed for work. Sometimes, I found him still sitting at the kitchen counter with Peter, and I joined them with a cup of coffee. Other times, Darius grabbed his messenger bag and headed out the door the minute I walked in.

Now, every evening, a little before six, Darius walked through the door just in time to join Peter and me for dinner. I'd fallen into the habit of cooking both Darius and Peter's favorite dishes for dinner. It was a pleasure watching them devour the meal. Darius often took charge of Peter after dinner, giving him a bath and getting him ready for bed while I washed up the dishes. Then Peter would rush down the stairs to hug me goodbye.

I'd made lasagna for dinner again tonight, but Darius had called to say he was going to be late. At least he'd called.

Johnathan would have blown me off completely. I'd already given Peter his bath, read him his favorite story, three times, and tucked him in. Now, as I sat on one of the sofa chairs in the living room, and the grandfather clock in the foyer chimed six forty-five, I heard the door leading to the garage open. Moments later, Darius walked into the living room.

"I'm so sorry," he greeted me, setting his bag down on the couch.

"No worries."

With the current traffic and the drive time, I'd be lucky if I made it home before eight. The drive didn't bother me though. It was the fact that I missed them already, and I had yet to walk out the door that chased my smile away.

"Are you good to drive?"

"Yeah, of course. Have you eaten? The lasagna's in the oven."

"I've been thinking about it all day."

I ignored the way my stomach dipped at the smile that spread across Darius's full lips.

"Okay, I'd best get going. I'll see you tomorrow."

He walked with me out the front door, down the steps to my small car parked in his circular driveway. He held my door open for me as I climbed in and started the engine.

"Drive safely."

"I will."

"And, text me when you get home?"

"Okay, I can do that." I laughed. His concern for my well-being warmed me to my bones. Heat flowed through my veins. But I didn't want him to worry.

"I'll see you in the morning."

He shut the car door and stepped back. His hands went to his side pockets, and he stood there, watching as I drove away. I glanced in the rearview mirror before I turned at the end of the driveway. He was still standing there, watching me leave.

I couldn't deny it any longer. I was attracted to Darius Peyton. He was handsome, driven, and caring. Not to mention he was easy on the eye. Okay, that was putting it mildly. The man was gorgeous and he hit all the right notes for me.

The problem was I wasn't looking for a quick fling with Peter's guardian. And I didn't kid myself into believing it was going to be anything other than a quick fling. Darius was just getting back to work after a three-month absence and he had his hands full running his business. But, I also suspected that even if he hadn't been preoccupied with Peter for months, he would still have his hands full. Darius was ambitious. There was nothing wrong with that. It just meant there was no room in his life for me. I would be a fool to get involved with him, because invariably I would want much more than he was willing to give.

"Look at you being all presumptuous." I chuckled in the quiet car.

This heat between us could be one way. What if I was the one feeling it and Darius was unaffected? Perhaps I was the only one experiencing butterflies in the pit of my stomach. Nah, I didn't think it was one-sided. I'd felt enough of the chemistry to know the electric current ran both ways. But I didn't doubt for a moment that I would be the one to feel the fallout.

And where would that leave me with Peter? I was his teacher, at least for the remainder of the year. I couldn't do anything to jeopardize my relationship with him. If Darius and I had a relationship and it ended, would I be able to face him at those regular parent-teacher conferences?

Yeah, I definitely wasn't going there.

I switched the radio on and turned the volume up so that

the chorus of *Jingle Bells* pushed out every thought from my mind. Forty-five minutes later, I was pulling into my parking spot in front of my apartment.

The red roses on the ground in front of my apartment door stopped me in my tracks. I looked around, but there was no one else in the hallway, or on the stairs. I picked up the bouquet, looking for a card. There was none.

"Johnathan."

I looked around.

There was no sign of him.

I wanted to drop the flowers on the floor and leave them there. Instead, I carried them into the apartment with me and placed them on the counter. Johnathan wasn't taking no for an answer. He intended to wear me down, hoping that I would give in and agree to start dating him again.

What would be the point though? I had zero interest in lost causes and any relationship with him would definitely be a lost cause.

And so would any relationship with Darius.

My sigh echoed through my empty apartment. After the day spent with Pete, this felt lonely in comparison. Lonely and empty. I enjoyed the time I spent with both Peter and Darius. I was attracted to Darius, but it would never work. We were opposites. He was a bachelor billionaire with a demanding job and a nephew to care for. He had his hands full and wasn't looking for anything long term. I was a teacher with a desire for a family of my own and I was already attached to Peter.

The best thing I could do for myself right now would be to focus on Peter and my commitment to caring for him through the end of the Christmas holidays.

This was his first Christmas without his parents. Had that realization sunk in for him yet? What would happen when it did? How would he handle it? My mind immediately thought of Darius. How was he handling the first Christmas without his brother and sister-in-law?

It couldn't be easy for either one of them. I wanted to be there to help them navigate it. Starting something romantic with Darius now would be a bad decision. It would only complicate things and get in the way. I couldn't risk that. Darius and I were better off as friends. That's all.

CHAPTER 12

DARIUS

"Have you thought about getting a Christmas tree?"
I paused; the cup of morning coffee in my hands halfway to my lips.

Ah..."A Christmas tree?"

"Yeah, you know, 'tis the season?" Hope laughed.

She sounded like musical bells tinkling in my ears; full of joy and happiness. I walked over to the kitchen sink and dumped the contents of my cup into the sink. Grabbing the sponge, I washed out the cup before placing it in the dish rack to drain.

Christmas. Of course. The holiday was just a little over a week away. The hooting train in the background was now pulling into the station. I wasn't ready at all. Taking a deep breath, I hoped to ease the tightness in my chest. Then I turned to face her.

Her expression dropped, the smile disappearing from her lips, the laughter dulling in her eyes.

"Hey, it's okay." She made a dismissive wave with her hand. "I know this is a difficult time for you and Peter. I just thought if our goal is to help him get back to a sense of normal, we should probably think about Christmas and getting ready for it. You know, teachers love to have their students give a report about their Christmas holiday. I'd hate for Peter to be put in an awkward position."

I leaned against the kitchen sink, crossing my ankles, and folding my arms against my chest. She was right.

"Christmas was Alice's favorite holiday. I swear she was Santa's helper. I want Peter to have a good Christmas, but there's no way I could do what Alice would have done for him."

She walked over to me and leaned against the sink. Her sweet apricot smell floated around me, begging me to come closer.

"Alice would never expect you to do that. She would only ever want you to do the best that you could do."

"My brother and I hated Christmas before Alice came along."

"Really? Why?"

I rubbed my palm over the nape of my neck, hoping to ease the tension I felt. "Well, it's like you said. Teachers love to ask kids what they did on their Christmas break. Shawn and I were usually stuck with the nanny while my parents were off on a business trip-turned-holiday getaway."

"Without you?"

She seemed flabbergasted at the idea. I nodded, holding her stare. I'd never opened up about my childhood to another woman. There hadn't been anyone that I'd been close enough to share something this intimate with. Shawn and I had talked about our childhood a lot, especially after Peter's birth when he had begun to understand the love a father had for his son, and the reality of what had been missing in our childhood had become crystal clear. Shawn had always been my go-to person. He'd been the one I could discuss my feelings with. I missed him so much. Holding Hope's stare, I searched for her emotions. I didn't want her pity. Luckily, I just saw concern and support, and something else that made my breath catch in my throat. I felt the space between us close a little.

"I want to do right by Peter. But I'm not sure I know how to. Will you help me?"

"Of course!"

She rested her hand on my shoulders. I felt her support and knew she was on my side. She cared about us. Sharing with her felt comfortable and right.

I reached out to hug her in gratitude, and she met me halfway, wrapping her arms around my shoulders and drawing me close to her. I'd hugged her instinctively, wanting to thank her for her friendship and her caring support, but all too soon the warmth of her body against mine, the wonderful smell of flowers and apricots that was so Hope, had awareness stirring inside of me, stealing my breath.

My hands felt wonderfully right against her back, and her curves fit me perfectly. Hugging Hope felt like coming home. A spark of arousal shot through me all the way to my groin.

"You smell great," I murmured, my face buried in her neck. I exhaled against her skin and felt the tremble that raced through her.

"You do too." Her voice sounded husky, sexy.

Reluctantly, I lifted my head, pulling away from her embrace. She released me, but she didn't step away. Neither did I. We were mere inches away from each other. Our gazes clashed, and I felt the heavy stirring of desire. I was quickly losing control of my body. To avoid embarrassing myself or her, I cleared my throat before attempting to speak.

She was a wonderful friend. I shouldn't risk that, and yet, I couldn't resist cupping her cheek in my large hand and stroking a thumb over her high-cheekbone.

"Thank you, Hope. I appreciate you, and I'm so grateful for everything you're doing to help Peter and me."

She wet her lips with the tip of her tongue. Her gaze dropped to my mouth for a moment, just long enough to cause the tension that already existed between us to tighten and hum like a twine pulled tight and about to snap.

What would her mouth feel like against mine?

What would she sound like when I kissed her, exploring every inch of her mouth until I knew the shape and feel by heart?

She shook her head, as if shaking off a fog. She leaned closer to me, parting her lips as if responding to my desire. "I should—"

"Can I watch *Paw Patrol*?"

We broke apart and whirled around to face our little intruder. Peter stood by the island, his face set in a determined line. Usually, I didn't like him watching TV so early in the morning, but today was the exception. Hope and I both needed another minute.

"Sure, Bud, but just one episode, okay?"

"Yay!" Peter fist-pumped the air and ran off to the living room, leaving us alone together again.

I cleared my throat, about to speak, but Hope beat me to it.

"I should check on him."

"Yeah, sure. I should get going myself."

We both moved in the opposite direction, but somehow ended up standing next to each other at the kitchen table. I smiled. She did too. It was weird — this tug toward each other, but I wasn't sure if it was altogether bad.

"So, about the Christmas tree." Hope shoved her hands in

the back pockets of her jeans. I tried not to focus on how the movement caused her sweater to draw closer against her chest.

"Yes, the Christmas tree." I grabbed my bag off the chair. "Alice would get a tree from a market in Richmond every year. She and Shawn made a big deal about blocking off that Saturday. Peter might be too young to remember, but he used to love it."

"Let's do it, then. Tomorrow."

"Yeah?"

"Yeah! How about ten tomorrow morning? I could come over and we could head over from here."

"You don't mind spending your Saturday morning with us?"

"Not at all."

"Okay. It's a date." She lifted her eyebrows at my word choice, then nodded, a smile playing across her mouth.

"Okay."

Moments later, I was out the door and pulling out of my garage in my work truck. I'd tossed out the word date and she hadn't protested. Excitement bubbled inside me at the thought of spending the morning with Hope and Peter. Christmas tree shopping at a Christmas tree market was going to be a first for me. One I couldn't wait to enjoy with Hope and Peter.

CHAPTER 13

DARIUS

I was in trouble.

"The nanny is off-limits."

That's what I'd told the guys. But I hadn't bargained on the push and pull between us growing stronger. I hadn't had to fight to keep myself from kissing her delicious lips, and wondering why the hell I shouldn't. Who knew I could yearn for a woman's kiss? I wanted to wrap her up in my arms, press her body against me, and seal her lips with mine.

I threw my pen down on my desk and pushed my chair back. Walking over to my window, I stared out at the view of Bellevue Park in the distance.

There was something more to Hope. She was more than Peter's nanny. More than just my friend. I didn't understand it. I'd been aware of her from the beginning. Attracted to her. I'd wanted more of a connection, but I'd resisted for Peter's sake. He had to come first, and I never wanted to do anything to jeopardize his well-being.

But…Hope!

There was no denying I wanted more. She mattered to me as a friend, but I was attracted to her as a woman. A woman I wanted very much. Being around her felt like awakening from a very long sleep. Longer than three months, if I was being honest. I'd been closed off and oblivious to this deep yearning all my life. I'd never felt anything like this with another woman. If I had, would I have ever promised myself to focus entirely on work and avoid any deep relationships with women? Or would I find myself being torn between a woman and work, much like Shawn had been?

Hope was unexpected. She had the potential to change everything. Did I want her to? That was the question.

Someone knocked on my office door. I turned around just as Brian pushed it open and stuck his head in.

"Got a minute?"

"Yeah, sure. Come on in." His interruption was a pleasant reprieve. I wasn't going to solve the dilemma of my budding feelings for Hope by pondering on it. Work was what I needed to focus on right now.

"What have you got?" I asked Brian as he walked over to join me in front of the windows.

"Spoke to Allen. He's willing to come into town for a meeting."

"Great!"

"Well." Brian smiled and shoved his hands into his pockets. "I hope you still think so when you hear the rest of it."

"What?"

"I invited him to dinner at your house."

"Dinner at my house? What in the world made you do that?"

"You're the closest thing this company has to stability now, Darius. It totally makes sense. If Shawn were alive, we would be meeting at his house with Alice and Peter in attendance."

"Shawn's not here."

"True, but you have a house and personal family obligations that point to your maturity and commitment. We can hire a chef for the evening. You're a single father. Surely, Allen wouldn't frown on you having help."

"So, basically, you want to use my four-year-old nephew to sweeten Allen up."

Brian hesitated. I thought he looked a little redder in the face when he shook his head and spoke again. "I'm sorry. It was a bad idea."

Some of my irritation flowed out of me at his apology. I sighed. "No. It's a damn good idea. Strategic. It gives Allen the image he's looking for. And Hayden is likely to be less insulting if Peter's in the room."

Brian's frown turned into a smile. He clasped me on the back. "I've arranged it for the week after Christmas."

"Fine. But have your assistant make the arrangements for a chef, will you? Planning a dinner is the last thing I want to deal with now."

"I'll have Sarah take care of everything."

"And now that I'm back at work full-time, I need an assistant."

"I'll have Sarah take care of it. I'm sure the temp agency can find us a good match."

I nodded. Walking over to the wet bar across the room, I poured myself a healthy dose of scotch and took a drink. I arched an eyebrow at Brian and lifted the bottle in his direction. He walked over to me with a nod. I poured scotch into another glass and handed it to him.

"Everything okay?" he asked after he'd taken a sip.

I mulled his question over in my mind, in no hurry to answer. Brian was patient. I needed to confide in someone about how I was feeling about Hope. Brian and Hayden were the closest people I had to friends. I already knew Hayden thought I ought to move Hope into my home. Of the three of us, Brian was most like Shawn, and I really needed my brother's advice right now.

I nodded, then took another sip of the liquid courage. "Things are...changing between Hope and me. I'm not sure what to do about it."

"Changing how?" Brian took another sip. His free hand disappeared into his pants pocket as he held the tumbler loosely in his hand. He stared into it, swirling it ever so slightly.

"My feelings for her are changing."

"Into?" he pressed.

"Something more than friendship."

He nodded. "It happens. What's the problem?"

"She's not someone I could mess up with. I have Peter to consider. She's his teacher, for God's sake. I would be an idiot."

"I hear a but."

"But I'm attracted to her."

Brian lifted his eyebrow but said nothing. "She's like a breath of fresh air that's moved through my life. I love having her around, and she's great with Peter. I just wish I wasn't so attracted to her. I don't want to do anything stupid. She's not the type to sleep around. And based on the comments she's made, I think she broke up with her ex-boyfriend because he wouldn't commit. I'm cut from the same cloth. Brian, you know me. Marriage, kids, that was Shawn. I'm not looking for that."

"Yet you have Peter, and you're doing a great job with him."

"Because I don't have a choice. He's my nephew, and he's all I have left of Shawn. I can't fail him. I would move heaven and earth to give him what he needs. But a committed relationship? Shit. That's even more than I can handle right now."

"Whoa." Brian held out his palm. "I think you're overanalyzing things. You're attracted to this woman, and she may as well be to you. But you're far from relationship and commitment talk. You guys aren't even dating. I think you need to take a deep breath and just go with the flow for a bit."

I nodded, but I didn't think Brian was right. He didn't see Hope and I together. How could he know about the sparks that were flying? The way it felt so right between us. He didn't have a clue about the familiarity and the comfort that came from being in the same room with her and sharing Peter's care with her. She was becoming ingrained in my life. And I was falling for her. My nephew's nanny.

"Yeah, you're right." I forced a smile for Brian and took another sip. I would have to Uber home if I kept this up. I didn't relish the thought of showing up to Peter and Hope slightly buzzed. Setting my unfinished drink down, I moved over to my desk and started packing up my things.

"It's been a while since I've been attracted to a woman. I'm out of touch, making a big deal about it."

Brian nodded, set his drink down too, and walked over to me. "That's right. This is a good thing. See where it goes. Enjoy it."

"Yeah, I will. We're going Christmas tree shopping tomorrow."

"You're what?" He shoved both his hands in his pockets.

"Christmas tree shopping. At that place out in Richmond where Shawn and Alice would get their tree. Hope and I are taking Peter there. She wanted us to decorate the house for Christmas. Timing's perfect, actually. It'll look good for Allen's dinner."

"Awesome." I saw him rub his chin with his index finger. I

ignored the look of speculation on his face and grabbed my messenger bag, heading for the door.

Brian had been the one convincing me a moment ago that I needed to go with the flow when it came to my attraction to Hope. Christmas tree shopping and decorating my house with her probably weren't the things he had in mind. It certainly wasn't anything either one of us had done with a woman before. But it was right up Hope's alley. Right about now, Brian was probably figuring out what I already knew: Hope wasn't like any woman I'd dated before. She was a keeper, and I was playing with fire by easing back and seeing where this thing between us went. But damn if I had any desire to stop myself.

CHAPTER 14

HOPE

"That's the one!" I exclaimed, pointing at the giant Christmas tree a few feet away that was entirely too big for the top of Darius's Jeep Wrangler. Peter pulled away from his uncle's hand and ran over to the tree.

"That one?" Darius jerked his thumb at the mammoth pine.

"Ahha." I nodded as I slowly approached the tree with the respect it deserved. "It's beautiful," I told Darius.

"Right." He rubbed his palm across the back of his neck before shoving his hands in his back pocket.

"Can we get it, Uncle Dar?"

Peter ran his little palm along the branch of needles and laughed at the tickling sensation. My heart fluttered at the sound of his laughter. I felt warmth flow through me and a smile settle on my mouth. I glanced back at Darius to find him watching me, and my words stuck in my throat under his silent perusal.

He looked at me differently now, after yesterday morning. There was heat in his eyes. Heat and something intense that made tingles go up and down my spine. I looked away because I felt it again. The certainty that we were both heading down unfamiliar territory. I was terrified of the ramifications of wanting what I could see Darius offering with his eyes.

Yesterday, I'd hugged him instinctively, wanting to offer comfort, but all too soon, the feel of my arms around his broad shoulders, his breath against my neck, the warmth flooding through my veins had left me breathless and wanting more than his hug. How long could we ignore this intense attraction for each other? How long before one of us made a move?

"Guys, this one's got to be at least twelve feet tall! How do you propose we get it back to the house?"

"Please, Uncle Dar? Please!"

"I'm not even sure it'll fit in the foyer."

"Have you seen your foyer?"

"You're not helping, Hope."

I laughed at the look of mock sternness on his face. Meanwhile, Peter had turned his full attention to the tree once more.

"I'm sure the farm offers a delivery and set-up service."

"They'd better. 'Cause there's no way it's fitting on top my jeep."

"You're buying it?"

"Of course, I am. If it can make Peter smile like that? Make you smile like that? Yeah, it's worth the hassle."

"That's so sweet; I think."

The corners of his mouth curled upwards and his eyes sparkled. "Hey, this is coming from a guy who's never purchased a Christmas tree in his life."

"Never? So, what did you do every year you were growing up?"

"Mother called a decorator. They brought everything over, and when it was time, they came and picked it up."

From the little I'd gathered about Darius's family, I suspected his mother had to get a professionally decorated tree because of all the social obligations she and her husband had, being business leaders in their community. I still felt a needle prick of sadness for the little boy who'd never experienced the joy of shopping for the perfect tree and then decorating it himself.

"Well, for your first Christmas tree ever, I'd say you've picked a winner."

We stood by the tree, claiming it, guarding it, until we could flag one of the attendants walking by. Only after we'd completed the purchase and arranged for their delivery company to drop it off home later this afternoon did we walk away from it.

"Can I interest you in a cup of coffee?"

"Sure, that sounds wonderful!"

"And what about you, Bud? How about a cup of hot chocolate?"

Peter bobbed his head in complete favor of getting a cup of his favorite drink. Darius swung Peter up onto his shoulders, much to his delight. We made our way to the front of the farm to where the coffee booth was. We were waiting for our drinks when I heard a man call my name behind me. I turned around and felt surprise hit me like a boulder.

"Johnathan." Uneasiness settled in my stomach at the sight of my ex standing in front of Darius and me. "What are you doing here?"

"Helping a friend grab a tree."

I felt a flutter of irritation at having to come face-to-face with his latest girlfriend, but then Johnathan did a chin nod to a man in his early twenties who was buying a hot dog at the booth next to the coffee shop. The guy was as muscular as Johnathan in a navy-blue denim and an oatmeal-colored sweater.

"Who's this?" Johnathan asked, looking squarely at Darius with Peter still perched on his shoulder. Johnathan's tone made me hesitant to reveal who Darius really was. Darius and I weren't a couple, but Johnathan clearly thought we were. It wasn't any of his business anyway, and he shouldn't be acting as if I was doing something wrong by being here with Darius and Peter, shopping for a tree. Yet, Johnathan clearly was.

"Darius Peyton." Darius held out his hand.

Johnathan took it. "Johnathan Fields."

They released hands, clearly happy to have the introductions out of the way. I was about to extricate ourselves from Johnathan when he suddenly took my elbow and led me away from the coffee booth, and Darius.

"Who is this guy?"

"A friend."

"I stopped by your apartment a couple times this week, but you weren't there."

"Why? I told you it was over."

"Because of him?"

"Because of you, Johnathan."

"I've changed. Give me a chance, and I can prove it to you."

"I'm sorry, it's not going to work. Goodbye, Johnathan."

I pulled away from him and walked back to Darius and Peter, just as the barista was handing Darius our drinks. I took the coffee from him and the three of us walked toward Darius's jeep. I climbed into the front while he buckled Peter into his car seat and placed his hot chocolate in the cupholder next to him. Only when Darius was driving away did he speak.

"The ex-boyfriend?"

I nodded, looking out the window.

"Is he the one that's been calling non-stop?"

Heat filled my cheeks. "He's having a hard time accepting my answer."

"Is he a problem?" The quiet tone in Darius's voice told me that my answer was going to dictate what happened next.

"No. Nothing I can't handle."

"You shouldn't have to handle him."

"It's okay. Really, it is. I think seeing us together finally drove home to Johnathan that I meant it when I said we were over. Not that I told him we were a couple or anything."

"Hope. It's fine."

I sighed and settled my head back against the headrest.

"Why did you two break up? He seems crazy about you."

"That's just the strangest thing. He wasn't when we were together. Far from it, actually." I didn't want to admit to a guy as gorgeous and sexy as Darius that my boyfriend had found me so lacking he'd hooked up with his co-worker while we were still dating. I glanced at Peter, who had fallen asleep in his car seat. So, I told him about running into Shawn and Alice at the restaurant instead.

"Seeing the two of them together reminded me of what I really wanted in a relationship, and it gave me hope that it truly did exist out there. I had to only wait for it."

"They were pretty amazing together."

"Yes."

"Shawn swore he wasn't going to fall in love, have children, and ruin a woman's life. He was too focused on Gemini. Then he met Alice. All bets were off."

He glanced at me, and I smiled. I could tell he was

remembering the love between his brother and his sister-in-law.

"She was all he could think about. She became the most important thing in his life. More than any new business deal or acquisition, he wanted her. He went out of his way to show her every day how much she meant to him, even after they were married. He did his best to put her first. They were celebrating their five-year wedding anniversary that night."

Darius drove in silence for a few minutes, lost in his memories of his brother and sister-in-law. Later, when he cleared his throat and I met his gaze across the console of the car, I saw the shine of unshed tears in his eyes.

"Peter and I are having lunch with my parents tomorrow. Will you come with me?"

"Your parents?" I laughed nervously.

"I could do with a friend at that table. I have no idea what I'm doing with Peter half the time, and my mother knows it. If I can show her I have support, that I'm not doing this alone, it might cause her to ease up a bit. You're Peter's teacher. They'll respect you. Please say you'll come. I could do with your support."

Was I seriously going to consider this? "Of course! I'm happy to help."

The smile that spread across Darius's face left my stomach in knots and my heart fluttering erratically. Warning bells sounded like alarms, causing me to put my back up. I was heading into dangerous territory. Darius and I were friends, but more importantly, I was working for him. He was paying me to take care of Peter. While I would have done it for free, because Peter was a pleasure, I was just the nanny he'd hired for the Christmas break.

Hanging out with them outside of my nanny hours could get complicated real fast. Especially when it felt so comfortable being with Peter and Darius. Not to mention that this moment — sitting next to him, with Peter asleep in the back, while he drove us home — smacked off my heart's desire come to life. I wanted a family of my own. Darius's request to have lunch with his family tomorrow hit so close to home. Everything about us was a minefield filled with emotions. I had to be careful where I stepped, or I would never survive the fallout.

CHAPTER 15

HOPE

"It's here!" Peter screamed from his spot at the window in the dining room where he had a clear view of the delivery truck driving up Darius's circular driveway.

Peter had been sitting at the window for the past half hour since the salesperson from the Christmas tree market had called to say that the truck was only thirty minutes away.

"So they are!" I said, snatching him up in a tight hug before allowing him to scamper off after Darius, who was already opening the front door.

The three of us stepped back as the men brought the giant Christmas tree inside. We watched; Peter in awe, and Darius and I in growing trepidation as they mounted the mammoth pine on its stand, made sure it was straight and balanced, and then wished us a Merry Christmas before leaving us to come to grips with the task ahead of us.

"Right." Darius rubbed his palm across the nape of his

neck and eyed the tree warily before turning to face me. "What did you talk me into?"

"Me? Why are you blaming me?"

"I seem to remember you encouraging him."

"Come on, it's not going to be that bad."

"I don't think we bought enough ornaments. We should probably just hire someone. I have no idea how many ornaments we need for this thing, but I'm pretty sure it's more than we bought."

"We could always pick some more up tomorrow."

"Or we could hire someone."

"It's more fun if we do it ourselves."

"I doubt that."

I burst out laughing. Darius looked skeptical. He'd pushed his sweater sleeves up, revealing the dusting of dark hair on his well-defined arms. I longed to feel those arms pulling me close to him again.

Peter reached out and grabbed our hands, startling me out of my daydreaming. "Can we decorate it now? Please?"

"Yes, we can!" I said, taking a step toward the tree.

Peter followed me. He ran his hand reverently over the fir on a branch. Behind me, Darius sighed. A moment later, he, too, was standing next to me in front of the tree.

"Okay. Fine. Let's do this." His voice vibrated with determination.

"We need a ladder."

"You think?" He smirked before walking away in the direction of the kitchen and toward the garage.

"Alexa, play Christmas music."

Soon the opening notes of *All I want for Christmas* floated through the speakers.

"Okay, Peter. Let's find the lights in the bags."

Together, Peter and I went through the bags of decorations we'd purchased on the way home, pulling out the boxes of clear, white Christmas tree lights. We found the last of the twelve boxes just as Darius walked in carrying a very tall ladder.

"That's perfect!" I praised him.

He nodded, setting up the ladder next to the tree.

"Here." I opened one of the boxes of lights and pulled it out. "Let's put the lights on first. Would you plug this in, please?" I handed him the end with the plug.

Soon the balled-up string of lights in my hand came to life.

"Wow!" Peter exclaimed, clapping his hands together. "I want one." He picked up one of the boxes, tearing into it. Darius laughed and walked over to Peter to help him open the box of lights.

I took the little black twisty off the bundle in my hand and unraveled the string of lights.

"We need to wrap this string around the branches. Let's start at the bottom and work our way up."

I began to wrap the string of lights in my hand around the base of the tree, going around and around, alternating between placing them deeper in against the trunk of the tree and out closer to the tip of the branches. When I ran out of string, Peter handed me his before running to get another box to tear into.

I plugged it in and unraveled the string. Darius held out his hand. I lifted my gaze to find him watching me with a soft smile on his face that caused my heart to bounce around in my chest. I handed the lights to him, and he tucked the dead end deep among the branches, hiding the connection from view, before wrapping the lighted string around the branches. He mimicked my action, going around in circles, higher and higher.

I took the bundle from Peter, unwrapped it, and handed the end to Darius. We continued this way — Darius wrapping the lights around the tree and Peter opening the boxes — until all the lights were done and the tree was beautifully lit.

"It looks perfect." I stepped back to eye the tree. We'd gotten just the right amount of lights.

"Not bad." Darius appeared at my side.

"For your first time," I teased, bumping my hip against his side.

He laughed, looking down at me. My breath hitched, and a shiver of pleasure raced up my spine. He looked so handsome, bathed in Christmas tree lights.

"The ornaments," I announced, moving away from Darius's tempting lips. "Peter, let's get the biggest ornaments out of the bags."

"Okay!" Peter started tearing through the bags, pulling out the larger ornaments.

I found the plug-in foot switch in one of the bags and swapped out our set-up so that the first strand was plugged into the foot switch instead. I placed it beneath the tree, within easy reach, and left the lights off.

The jolly sounds of *Let It Snow!* filtered through the speakers as we placed the large round ornaments on the bottom branches. Deciding earlier to stop by the higher end craft tech store on the way home had been a winner. The crystal faux glass balls picked up the twinkling lights from the tree. The red, green, and gold ornaments were traditional, but perfect for Peter and Darius's first Christmas tree.

I watched as both of them placed the ornaments on the tree. I only had to go behind them a couple times, spacing out the ornaments when Peter put them too close to each other. Soon, Darius was climbing the ladder and tucking the smaller ones higher up on the top of the tree.

Three hours later, Peter and I stood back as Darius

climbed the ladder one more time to put the large angel at the top.

"Ready?" I asked when he was safely on the ground again.

"Ready!" both he and Peter said in unison.

I stepped on the foot switch. The tree lit up. Peter clapped and cheered.

"It's perfect," I exclaimed.

Darius stood, staring at it in awe. Then his gaze dropped to Peter and his obvious delight before connecting with mine.

Thank you, he mouthed the words over Peter's head.

I nodded.

"Do you like it, Bud?" He swung Peter into his arms and took a step toward the tree.

"I love it!" Peter fingered one of the clear glass ornaments we'd purchased today.

"Not bad at all for our first Christmas tree." I smiled at Darius as I ruffled Peter's hair.

"Not bad at all," Darius echoed.

The three of us stood there for a moment, staring at the tree and what we'd created together.

"Do you know what we need?" Darius leaned closer to my ear and whispered.

"What?"

"Dinner. Can you stay?"

I glanced at my watch and grimaced. It was already going on eight o'clock at night. I should leave now if I wanted to make it home before nine. Only, the desire to stay and have dinner with Darius and Pete was so strong that it stifled logic and made it impossible to say no.

"Sure. I'm sure I can pull something together."

"Nope. I've got it." Darius pivoted in the direction of the kitchen, still carrying Peter with him. I followed, watching in silent amusement as he deposited Peter on a stool next to the island and then walked over to the fridge, pulling it open to study its contents.

Moments later, leftover lasagna was in the microwave and he was emptying a bagged Caesar salad into a large bowl.

"Not bad. I'm impressed," I complimented him when we were sitting at the table a short while later, about to dig into the dinner he'd assembled.

"Years of being a bachelor. I'm a master at pulling together leftover dinners."

"Another lifetime?" I teased him.

"Yeah. For sure." He smiled at me across the table.

We both noticed Pete's head falling to his chest before he caught himself.

"Looks like time for bed for you, Bud."

Peter pushed away from the table without complaint. Darius and I both laughed. He must really be tired if he wasn't resisting. I glanced at my watch and grimaced.

"I should get going as well." It was already after nine o'clock.

"Hope?"

"Yes." I turned to face Darius who was once more carrying Peter on his hip. My heart fluttered at the sight of the two of them together. They were so handsome. They looked so right together. Everything I desired.

"Why don't you stay the night? It's late and I don't like the idea of you driving home this time of night."

Stay the night? My eyes widened. Warmth flooded through me, and my breath caught in my throat.

"I could make up the guest bedroom for you."

"Oh." Heat exploded in my cheeks. "Sure. Okay. If it's not too much trouble for you."

"Great. How about we get this sleepyhead down to bed and then we'll get you settled?"

"Sounds like a plan." I smiled to hide the butterflies that had taken flight in my stomach.

Darius was being thoughtful, and I was being stupid, getting all worked up. It was late and I knew he felt uncomfortable with my long drive. Of course, he'd offered me one of his guest bedrooms. It was silly of me, getting nervous about the idea of spending the night in the same house as Darius. Silly and immature. Yet, knowing this didn't stop my heart from beating irrationally, or me from feeling flushed, like I'd stepped too close to the fireplace.

We got Peter ready for bed as quickly as we could. After we'd both kissed him goodnight and tucked him in, I followed Darius out of Pete's bedroom.

I suddenly felt bone-tired. "Thank you for letting me crash here tonight. I appreciate it."

"No problem at all. I'm glad you said yes." Darius moved down the hall and opened a door to a bedroom. "Here you go." He stepped aside to let me in.

The room had white walls and furniture with navy blue accents. The king-sized bed sat in the middle of the room against the wall. Two white wingback chairs with navy blue accent pillows sat at the foot of the bed facing the wall with a large flat screen television mounted on it.

"This is lovely," I said, moving to the window and peeking out at the front driveway and the tall oaks surrounding the house.

"Everything you need should be in the linen closet in the bathroom. Did you want me to get you a t-shirt for tonight?"

"No, that's all right." I was sure my cheeks were as red as embers.

He paused, and I swear his gaze roamed over my body before connecting with mine again. "Right. Well, okay. I'll see you in the morning, then."

"Good night."

"Good night, Hope."

I watched as Darius turned and walked out of the bedroom, pulling the door closed behind him. Only then did I exhale, releasing the pent-up feelings that had risen to the surface. There was no denying it. No ignoring it either. I was attracted to him. Not just as Peter's guardian, but as a man. He was kind, thoughtful, smart, not to mention fun to be around. I never felt like a third wheel or an inconvenience when we were together. He was always a perfect gentleman. It also helped that he was handsome as hell. What was there not to like about Darius?

I knew he felt the undercurrents flowing between us. It was clear that he felt some kind of attraction for me. We were both denying it. Not for the first time today, I wondered how long could this continue before one of us acted on this intense attraction between us? Would I resist if Darius made a move on me? Would I want to? And if I gave in, would it ruin our friendship? Was I ready to take that chance?

CHAPTER 16

DARIUS

I was nervous.

The three of us were standing in front of my parents' front door and I wanted to usher Hope and Peter back to my car and ride out of there. We could go window shopping instead, watching all the Christmas decorations through the storefronts. Pete would love that, and it would feel a whole lot safer than bringing him to my mother's.

The door swung open, and my mother stood in front of us. I saw her assessment before she smiled and stepped back politely, allowing us into her frosty foyer.

"You're right on time. How lovely. And you're Ms. Martinez, aren't you? Peter's teacher? So nice of you to join us."

I watched Hope and my mother shake hands and had the unhealthy urge to yank Hope away from her. Helen Peyton was not a nice woman, and I didn't want Hope anywhere near her.

"You have a beautiful home." Hope smiled at my mother as she handed her leather jacket to the maid who had silently materialized next to us. I took my coat and Peter's off too and handed them both to the woman I'd never met before. The faces were always new. Mother had a high-turnover rate when it came to her household staff.

"Where's Father?"

"Called away, I'm afraid. It'll just be us for lunch today."

Big surprise! I realized I was clenching my jaw and told myself to relax lest I broke my molars. Some things just didn't change. I'd been foolish to expect that my father would want to have lunch with us. I didn't bother to ask any more questions about his whereabouts. It was all pointless anyway. I caught myself rubbing the back of my neck and shoved my hands in my back pocket instead, aware that my mother hated my restless gestures. I was on the edge of bolting, however. I wanted the hell out of here.

Hope reached out and squeezed my arm briefly as we followed my mother into the dining room. I looked over at her and saw the small smile she offered me. I reached for her hand and held on to it, allowing the warmth of her fingers to thaw the icy feeling in my chest.

Peter was oblivious to my mother's lack of warmth or attention. He held on to my hand and walked with us to the dining room even as he weaved his toy superhero through the air as if it were a toy plane. He was all that mattered. I'd made a silent promise to Shawn and Alice the night they died. I was never going to break that promise. Peter was mine to take care of.

We'd just been served the food when my mother asked, "Have you given any thought to Peter's return to school in January?"

"What do you mean?"

"Kingsley Academy for Boys is still accepting

applications. We should move quickly if we want Peter to start there this January."

I swore I saw red. I clenched down hard on the napkin in my lap and dragged it and my closed fist onto the table next to my plate. I held on to the napkin, giving me something to squeeze, when all I wanted to do was grab Peter and Hope's hands and get the hell out of here.

"I have no intention of enrolling Peter in a boarding school."

"Kingsley Academy is one of the best schools in the country. You and Shawn both flourished there. I would think Shawn would want his son to follow in his footsteps were he here to make the decision himself."

Well, that showed how much she knew. "If Shawn and Alice were alive, I know for a fact they would never put their four-year-old son in a boarding school, in another state."

"Shawn and Alice would want Peter to have the best education possible."

"He has the best education, Mother, right here."

Her pinched expression spoke volumes about what she thought about Silsbee Academy. She glanced at Hope and smiled before blotting her lips with her napkin and placing it next to her plate. I guessed she had also lost her appetite.

"We can talk about it later," Mother said.

"No, we wouldn't. This isn't something that's up for discussion."

Her expression said otherwise, and I felt my anger boil over.

"Shawn and Alice named *me* as Pete's guardian because they both knew I would raise him the way they would. I don't need your input, Mother, not when it goes against their wishes."

"We have to consider what's best for Peter." She ignored everything I'd just said.

"Thanks for the lunch. It was a pleasure as always." I pushed my chair backward, reaching for Peter. Hope was already coming to her feet across the table from me.

"Oh, for goodness's sake, Darius, sit down."

"No. We're done here."

We got our jackets, and I carried Peter out of my childhood home with Hope walking beside me. My mother stood in the open doorway, watching as I buckled Peter into his car seat and held the passenger door open for Hope to get in. I didn't spare my mother a single glance as I got into the car and drove away. Nevertheless, I sensed her unspoken promise — there would be repercussions.

Icy tentacles crawled along my spine. Shit! My mother wasn't an enemy I was looking forward to having, but sending Peter away to school was out of the question. Raising Peter wasn't going to be a joint venture between us. I had to shut her down, soundly and completely, because subtle didn't work with her. Unfortunately, it didn't take much to offend her, and I hadn't given a shit if I had. So, of course I had offended her. Big time.

Anger rode me hard, but so did the fear and anxiety I felt at the idea of losing Peter. I didn't want to fight with my mother over him, but I would never give in to her antiquated ideas of how to raise a kid. Why would she have even suggested that school? Shawn and I had hated it there. What made her think she had the right to suggest I put Peter in a boarding school?

I turned onto the San Luis Pass Road and drove along the ocean until I turned onto a street leading to Pirates Beach, and the three-story beach house that I hadn't visited in months. I pulled into the car park and turned off the car. A quick glance in the back seat confirmed that Peter was asleep. I took a deep, steadying breath and then turned to face the woman sitting silently beside me.

"I'm sorry," I murmured. She'd gotten pulled along into my drama with my mother and she'd barely said a word.

Now she sat facing me, completely at ease with having been driven to a strange place by a silent man struggling to contain his anger at his mother.

"This is our company's beach house. I should have asked your permission before driving you here. I need to clear my head, though. And, truthfully, I didn't want to be alone."

"It's okay. I'm sorry about your mom."

"I should have expected it. She's got her own ideas about how I should be raising Peter."

"You're doing a great job with him. He's happy, despite having lost the best part of his world. That's only because of you."

"And you." I reached across the console and took her hand. Peter was doing much better since Hope had begun watching him during the day. I'd kept him out of school after his parents' death because I'd barely been able to function in my own grief. He'd been so withdrawn and depressed, I hadn't had the heart to drop him off to school every day. It hadn't dawned on me how much he would miss his teacher, and how well he would do just by having Hope in his life.

"Hope," I continued, because she was shaking her head, and I knew she was about to dismiss her impact on Peter's life. My life. "You're the best part of our lives. I mean it. You've brought joy back into our lives."

"Oh, Darius." She rested her head back against her headrest. I held her stare and saw the flash of desire that looked a lot like my own.

I touched my palm to her cheek; felt her softness. "Thank you," I whispered.

"You're welcome." Her voice was husky and full of emotion. It stroked my spine and sent tingles racing over my skin. I swallowed my desire and tried to hold on to my resolve despite the intense urge to kiss her.

Pulling on my door handle, I stepped out of my car.

"Come on."

Carrying a sleepy Peter in my arms, I led the way to the elevator. The doors opened on the second floor to a sunny living room area. I placed Peter down on the couch and stepped aside as Hope spread a throw blanket over him.

I nodded toward the kitchen area, and she followed me, walking away from Pete with a backward glance.

"I'm sorry about the way things ended today."

"Who says it has to end?" She smiled. "I noticed you hardly ate a bite. Are you hungry?"

I did a gut check and nodded. "I could eat."

"Well, how about you whip out that black card of yours and order us something?"

I grinned. Reaching for my wallet, I asked, "What are you in the mood for?"

She glanced out the windows over the sink at the ocean outside before looking at me again, a smile on her lips. "Seafood seems appropriate."

"You got it."

Hope wandered off while I placed the order. I found her outside on the balcony of the living room. She was leaning against the wooden railing. The wind tousled her hair, lifting it and tossing it to and fro like feathers. She had a smile on her face as she took in the unobstructed scene of the white sandy beach and the choppy white-capped waters in front of her.

"This is truly beautiful."

"Like you," I murmured.

Her head snapped to me, and I held her stare. I saw the color sweeping up her neck to bloom in her cheeks.

"Thank you."

"Thank you for coming with me today."

"Thank you for inviting me."

"My mother can be unpredictable."

"She wants what's best for you and Peter."

I snorted. "I wouldn't go that far. She wants what's best for her image, and her idea of what the Peyton brand should be."

"So, you and your brother went to boarding school?"

"Most of our lives. My parents were busy. We had nannies when we were home on the holidays, but the rest of our time was spent away at school."

"That sounds lonely."

"It was." I leaned my back against the railing next to her and crossed my ankles. "The only thing she and my father did right was send Shawn and me to the same school. At least we had each other."

I pushed my hands in my pockets and stared at the little boy on the sofa inside the living room.

"I know for a fact Shawn wouldn't want that life for Peter. Alice sure as hell wouldn't. She was the best thing to happen to him. She taught him how to love. She was normal, and good, and all about life. She would nurture her son, hold him when he needed it, and hug him even when he didn't. She would not ship him off to another state to live, and certainly not at four years old."

"Pete is lucky to have you." Hope was holding her hair away from her face. Her eyes sparkled in the afternoon sun.

"We feel like the lucky ones."

She laughed in that dismissive way of hers that begged you not to focus on her. "Hope, I mean it. You're amazing. You're kind and patient. A true friend."

Her gaze dropped to my lips, causing my heartbeat to race in excitement. Hope made me feel alive again. No, not again. Just alive, period. I'd had entanglements with women before, but none of them had ever made me feel this way. None of them had made me burn with so much...want.

We were inches away from each other, standing in front of one of my favorite views. All I wanted to do was taste her. Why was I denying myself her kiss again? Hell if I could remember.

I lowered my head until I was mere inches from her mouth, never breaking eye contact with her. I waited for her to object. If she looked away or shifted from me, I would stop. I would brush it off, and we would continue. She didn't. A moment later, I closed the distance between us and captured her mouth with mine.

Kissing Hope felt like coming home after a long, rough travel. It was sweet yet explosive, comfortable but arousing all at the same time. It felt right. I shifted so that she was leaning against me, her body pressed closely to mine. I caressed her cheeks, tangled my hand through her long silky hair, and slanted my mouth to claim more of her, deepening that kiss so that I didn't know where I stopped and she began.

Heat rushed south and tore a groan from my lips. I swallowed her answering moan and pulled her against me. My hesitant exploration of her mouth gave way to barely leashed passion as she opened for me, giving me access to more of her: her passion, her desire, her!

I heard the car pull to a stop and lifted my head, breaking our kiss. We were both panting. I stared into her eyes, lost in the passion and want I saw there. She regained control of her desire for me. Her breathing evened out. I should apologize for kissing her, but I couldn't bring myself to utter the lie. I wasn't sorry.

"Food's here."

Her pupils were dilated. Her chest rose and fell against mine. She straightened and stepped away from my body. I felt the tremor that went through her, and I dropped my hands to her bare arms, caressing them.

"I'll get it." Hope bounced away from me and back into the house. She opened the front door just as the delivery man appeared. I rushed over to give him a tip. Hope had already placed the Styrofoam boxes on the island and was pulling out the paper plates and plastic spoons from the paper bag.

"Should we wake Peter?"

"No, let him rest."

We sat at the kitchen island with our plates in front of us and began eating in silence. Occasionally our gazes collided, and we smiled, but neither one of us said anything about the kiss or how it changed everything. Or how right it felt. We'd given in to the undercurrents flowing back and forth between us. Temptation. Desire. We'd finally stopped resisting the inevitable. I knew she had questions, just like I did. Chief among them being the question, what happened now? Having tasted her, felt her in my arms, how was I supposed to pretend that she didn't matter to me as someone more than just Peter's nanny? I didn't have a clue.

What did it mean for our arrangement? I studied her beneath my lashes as I took a bite of the fresh snapper. Her cheeks were flushed a delightful pink. She chewed thoughtfully as if she, too, was lost in thought about what we had just done.

"Hope, about that kiss." I placed my fork down in my Styrofoam container.

"Yeah, we should probably talk about that, shouldn't we?" Her gaze devoured my face, stopping on my lips again in a way that had my cock stirring in response.

"Yeah, we should. I think you're amazing and –"

"But we're just friends."

"What?" I paused, feeling like I'd just taken a plunge in the cold ocean outside my door.

"I know what you're going to say. You and I are such good friends. And Peter is so important to both of us. We don't want to complicate things."

"Ah…" I rubbed my palm against the nape of my neck. I hadn't been about to say any of that, but she was right. It was why I'd resisted kissing her all this time. But today, I'd chucked every sane reason and gone for it. And made a fool of myself in the process.

"Yes, you're right." I closed my box of food and shoved it across the table. "I hope you wouldn't hold this against me." I forced myself to meet her gaze, unwilling to hide from my foolish mistake.

"I don't. I have nothing but great respect for you and what you're doing for Peter. I'm here for both of you. I hope you know that."

"I do."

I smiled, grateful that she was being so graceful rather than running for the hills.

"Uncle Dar?" Pete called out. We both turned around to see him sitting up.

"Hey, Bud. How are you doing?" I pushed away from the table and strode over to him, thankful for the escape. I picked him up, wrapping him against my body.

He was the most important person in the room. I told myself he had to be, even as my gaze sort Hope out of its own accord, roaming over her face and connecting with her gleaming eyes. She was right. We needed to stay focused on Peter, not the crazy, hot desire running back and forth between us.

"Are you hungry, sweetheart?"

Peter nodded, and I took him over to the table and the baked red snapper, wild rice, and green beans we'd saved for him.

This simple meal with Hope and Peter, and the sounds of

the waves in the background, was a far cry from my mother's meal. The atmosphere here was warm, inviting, and it satisfied me as much as the meal did. That wasn't something I would have been able to say if we'd stayed at my mother's house.

Later, when Peter was finished eating, we took him for a walk on the beach. Hope and I walked alongside each other as Peter skipped ahead of us, picking up shells on the beach. When our bodies gravitated too close to each other and bumped, neither one of us said anything. Or moved away. Our time together was simple and satisfying. This was a memory I would never forget. What had started as a nightmare day had morphed into one of the most perfectly satisfying days of my life.

CHAPTER 17

HOPE

The days following our Sunday at the beach house passed like a dream, and before I knew it, we were only five days away from Christmas.

If I expected it to be weird between Darius and me because we'd kissed, I was pleasantly surprised to find that we seemed closer after our shared intimate moment at his beach house.

That man knew how to kiss. Any doubts I'd had about my decision to break up with Johnathan and wait for something more were gone like the sand being washed out by the ocean. This was passion. *Good bones.*

Kissing Darius had made me feel so *alive*. Alive with wanting and feeling wanted in return. His kiss had been everything. And it had scared me. I didn't want to experience this side of Darius, only to have to walk away at the end of the holiday.

So, I'd lied. I'd let him believe that our kiss hadn't changed everything. I'd told him that it hadn't affected me, hadn't mattered even though it had sent my heart beating wildly in my chest, and had turned me on, making me want more. I'd told him we were just friends, and I didn't want that to change. I think he believed me, though, I couldn't, for the life of me, understand *how* when I could *feel* the desire pulsing back and forth between us even now.

The three of us seemed to exist in our own bubble. We ate breakfast together, and more often than not, Darius made it home in time for us to have dinner together before I headed out. Then the next day, we did it all over again.

I should have been exhausted with the routine, but I was only ever anxious to wake up and drive over to his house again. I loved being with Pete. He was a smart boy, who was eager to learn, and he kept me on my toes. He had a natural love of learning, which made it fun and exciting to do projects with him, read, or just hang out at the complicated play structure in McKnight Grove Park, not far from Darius's house.

Once a week, I would drive Pete to his counselor's office for play therapy. Darius met us there and he and I would sit in the waiting room and chat, while Pete's therapist, Nadia Miller, worked with him. Peter always left in good spirits. The deep melancholy that had hung around him when I'd walked into his bedroom two weeks ago, was gone. He still had bad days when I could tell he was depressed or sad, but those days were few and far between, and his bouts with depression were short.

I was falling for Peter. Every day that passed brought me closer and closer to him. He was wrapping himself around my heart. I didn't want to think about what I would do when the holidays were over and his full-time nanny started. I loved my time with Peter, and it was going to break my heart when I didn't have to watch him anymore.

I found him sitting in the living room staring at the Christmas tree. I remembered the excitement of decorating it. It was an experience the three of us would never forget. I think it bonded us together.

"Are you okay?" I sat next to him on the carpeted floor and folded my legs beneath me.

He kept staring at the tree. After a while, he nodded. I recognized the pain on his face though.

"Do you miss your mom and dad?"

He nodded and pulled his knees up to his chest, resting his forehead on his knees.

"I know, sweetheart. I do too." I wrapped my arm around his shoulder and pulled him closer to me. There were no words to try to make him feel better. His pain was legitimate and there would be no brushing it off or hurrying it along. I sat with him in my arms and waited for the sadness engulfing him to pass.

After a moment, I felt him squirm in my arms. I loosened my hug. "How about we get out of the house for a bit?" I asked him. "We could go visit Santa's Village. Would you like that?"

I thought of the display at the mall, complete with Santa Claus and his elves. It might cheer Pete up to visit Santa and tell him what he wanted for Christmas.

Pete perked up instantly at the thought of going to the mall to visit Santa. I dialed Darius's cellphone as Pete and I went upstairs to brush his teeth and get him ready to leave the house.

"Hope, everything okay?"

"Yes. I'm sorry, am I disturbing you?"

"No, not at all. What's going on?"

I ignored the way his voice seemed to soften and lower as he spoke to me. It was so intimate that it reminded me of his kiss.

"I, ah, I'm taking Peter to see Santa at the village display in the mall."

"Is that a good idea? It's going to be crowded."

"He's been down all morning, and I think it'll cheer him up to get out of the house for a bit."

"Okay, I'll meet you at the second floor, south entrance, in an hour."

"You don't have to do that." Is that why he thought I'd called? I knew he was busy at work. I didn't expect him to shuffle his daily appointments around for me.

"It's not a big deal. Use the Jeep."

Darius hung up before I could protest. Was he upset with me? Or just in a hurry to get going? Pete finished brushing his teeth. I grabbed a comb and passed it through his hair. Then I found his black boots and pulled them on over his socks. I got out his heavy jacket and a beanie cap to cover his head. I was about to wrap a shawl around his neck when he ducked away from me and ran off. Okay, maybe the shawl was overkill. It was only in the lower sixties. Nevertheless, I carried it with us as we went down the stairs.

Moments later, Pete was buckled into his car seat in the back of Darius's Jeep Wrangler, and we were pulling out of his garage. It wasn't the first time I'd driven Darius's fancy ride. But it was the first time that his request for me to do so bothered me. Why had he wanted me to use his Jeep? Was he ashamed of my old beat-up sedan? I'd bought it second-hand in high school when I'd gotten my license and it had seen me through graduation as well as four years of college.

As I flipped the heat in the car and the leather seats began to warm up, I thought it might not be a bad idea to look into a newer vehicle. I had some money saved and I could find a cash car that would be better than my current situation.

Heat climbed up my neck and into my cheeks. Was Darius embarrassed by my car? By me? Johnathan had never wanted to be seen in my car. I was traditional enough to let the man drive when we went out on dates and Johnathan had never spared my Camry a second look.

But Darius wasn't a mean person, and he wasn't anything like Johnathan. Maybe Darius was taking care of me by asking me to drive his Jeep instead of my old car. That thought had me flushing and not in embarrassment. Or maybe he was just being a good *friend*. Ugh! That word! Hated it.

I had to circle the second-floor parking garage three times before I found a parking spot. I helped Pete out of the car, and with a tight hold on his hand, we walked toward the entrance. We had made it in just under an hour, so we found a spot out of the way and waited for Darius.

It wasn't long before I saw him walking toward us. He looked like a businessman out of a magazine in his blue dress shirt and gray trousers. The top two buttons were undone, and he'd left his tie and jacket at the office or in his car. His midnight black hair was wavy and looked soft like silk. He attracted more than a few stares from the women walking by, but he seemed oblivious to their attention.

I knew the moment he spotted us. I felt the jolt go straight through my body like an electrical current pulsing to life. A slow smile spread across his lips. It was masculine and cocky and attractive and sexy all at the same time. Oh. My. God! I already knew how good of a kisser he was, and in that moment, I wanted to feel his lips on mine again.

"Hi," he said, swinging Pete into his arms and bending down to plant a swift kiss on my cheeks.

Heat exploded where his lips had touched me and in other parts of my body too. I swayed toward him before I caught myself.

"Hi." I cleared my throat so I wouldn't sound so breathless, then I continued, "You were right. It's packed."

"Five days till Christmas!" He laughed.

"This might take longer than expected. It's okay if you need to get back to the office."

He shook his head. "I cleared my calendar for the afternoon."

"You did?" I knew he was in the middle of a big project at work.

He nodded. He must have sensed my surprise because he looked down at me, met my gaze for a brief second and then reached for my hand, taking it in his as we weaved through the holiday shoppers.

"I wouldn't miss this moment for anything."

He was putting Pete first, and it made all the difference in the way I saw him. I was sure Darius was an ambitious guy, like Johnathan, and he probably faced the same temptation to sacrifice time in relationships to get ahead in business. He'd just proven to me he knew how to put the people he cared about ahead of his financial gains.

My attraction to him kicked up a notch. I tightened my hold on his hand and let him navigate us through the crowds until we got to Santa's Village. The line to see Santa was long, but not as long as I thought it would be. Soon Peter was sitting on Santa's lap.

"Ho, ho, ho! Little Peter. I hear you've been a very good boy this year. Tell me, what would you like me to bring you this year?"

"Can you bring back my mom and dad?"

I lost my breath as my heart clenched painfully. I grabbed on to Darius's arm to hold him back when he would have climbed the stairs and enveloped Pete in his arms. I glanced at Darius and saw his lips pressed tightly together in a grimace. His shoulders were hunched over, and he looked devastated.

Santa saw the expression on both of our faces and was smart enough to realize it wasn't a possible request.

"Well, I'm afraid that's not a wish I can grant, son."

Pete nodded. "I didn't think so. Can you do a Lego set?"

Darius and I both nodded at Santa.

"Ho, Ho, Ho! You bet I can."

Satisfied, Pete ran over to us with a huge grin on his face. Darius picked him up and hugged him close. A moment later, he settled him on his hip.

"All set?" Darius smiled at his nephew, despite the tears in his eyes. I placed my hand on Darius's back, hoping he felt my support.

"Yep!" Pete reached over and hugged me, unexpectedly.

I planted a kiss on his cheek before he pulled away. I caught a couple stares from people walking by. And felt a tingle of happiness bursting forth. I knew what people saw when they saw us together. They thought we were a beautiful family. Pete's smiling face was enough to light up the world. The twinkle of joy and satisfaction in Darius's eyes made me feel ten feet tall, knowing I had something to do with it. There was also a comfortable familiarity between Darius and me that went beyond a nanny/boss relationship. Or even a friendship?

"How about something to eat?"

"Ice-cream!" Pete yelled.

"Actually, Bud, I was thinking about food. What do they have around here?"

"How about Little Bartholomew's?" I pointed to the American cuisine restaurant, not far from us, which was a smaller-sized, more affordable version of Bartholomew's on the Bayou.

"Sounds good."

Minutes later, we were seated at a table and looking at a

menu. The waiter came and took our orders. Peter was busy coloring on his menu. Darius smiled at me.

"Thank you."

"For?"

"Suggesting this. I'd forgotten about visiting Santa."

"You're doing a great job, Darius, balancing work and Peter."

He leaned closer to me. His voice was soft and serious when he spoke.

"I never wanted this. I was afraid my kid would always get the short end of the stick. Shawn and Alice made it look easy, but I knew it wasn't. I saw Shawn torn between choices, and always doing his best to make sure Alice and Pete knew how important to him they were."

We both looked at Peter who was busy coloring. Shawn had succeeded. It was why his death mattered so much to his son.

"You're doing a great job with him," I told Darius again, because I wanted it to sink in.

"It's gotten better and that's mostly thanks to your presence in our lives."

Pleasure coiled in my chest and burst into a warm, fuzzy feeling. It was nice to hear his words of praise.

"I don't know what we'll do when school starts for you."

I frowned. "Peter will be in school too, wouldn't he?"

"Yes. It's nice that he'll be in your classroom. I think it'll help him transition back to school." He looked across the table at Pete who was still busy coloring. "He's doing well, though, isn't he?"

"Yes. He is."

"Thank you, Hope."

He was giving me more credit than was due. I smiled and was about to shake my head and tell him it wasn't me when he reached for my hand and held it in his. I remembered the man who'd walked into my classroom almost two weeks ago. He'd looked haggard and worn around the edges. By contrast, today Darius was clean-shaven, and he looked at ease and well rested. He was handsome, and judging by the causal glances he was getting from women who walked by, I wasn't the only one who noticed. Darius was doing well too. Had that also been on account of our time together?

"You're welcome."

"Got any plans for Christmas?"

I needed to call my mom to make sure we were still on for lunch on Christmas Day, but other than that, I had no plans.

I shook my head. Darius smiled. "Any chance you'll spend the holiday with us? I'm off on Christmas Eve and the day after Christmas. We could do something together those three days."

"Would it involve your mother?"

"Absolutely not!"

I laughed. "Then, yes, I'd love to spend the holidays with you and Peter."

CHAPTER 18

DARIUS

I leaned against the kitchen sink, a cup of coffee in my hand, waiting for Hope to come downstairs from putting Pete to bed. Tonight, he'd wanted Hope to give him a bath and read him a bedtime story before tucking him in. It meant it was going on eight o'clock and she was still here. A quick glance at the kitchen clock confirmed she would be driving home, alone, late, in a car that I wasn't 100% sure would get her there. I could ask her to take the jeep and rest a little easier, knowing she stood a better chance of making it home without incident. Or I could just ask her to sleep in the guest room again.

Hope, in my guest bedroom, right down the hall from me. Was I trying to complicate things? I was already so attracted to her. And this pull between us had only grown stronger since our kiss on Sunday. She'd tried to play our kiss off as unimportant, but I saw the way she looked at me when she thought I wasn't paying attention to her. As if I wasn't always homed in on her when she was around. She was like a beacon calling to me, with her warmth, her kindness, her beauty.

Things were already complicated between the two of us. There was no pretending otherwise. So, what now? Did I take the chance and ask her for more? Would she say yes? Or would she turn me away? What would it do to Peter if things between Hope and I went sideways? Was that a risk I could take?

I set my coffee cup down in the sink behind me. My disappearance from work today meant I had to spend some time tonight in my home office, catching up with my part of the work that was due. I didn't mind. When I'd answered Hope's call today and heard her plans to take Pete to see Santa, I'd wanted to be there. It hadn't been hard to cancel everything, get in my truck, and drive over to the Galleria Mall.

Shawn and Alice used to take Pete to visit Santa's Village. Shawn would tell me all about Pete's reaction to Santa. I remember Shawn taking off from work, excited for the outing. It had been easy for me to make the decision to go with them today. It had been wonderful walking around the mall with Hope and Peter. I used to think I couldn't have a family and still achieve everything I wanted to at work. Then I'd watched, silently rooting for my brother as he attempted it. Now, I felt like I was carrying on with his dream. Only, sometime in the last month, it had become my dream too. Maybe, just maybe I could have it all.

I heard her footsteps on the stairs moments before she came around the corner. She smiled her gorgeous smile that curved her full lips upward and lit up her eyes. I held my hand out. Her gaze dropped to my hand before she walked across the room and took it.

"Thank you for taking such good care of him."

"He's so wonderful. It's my pleasure."

"It was a great idea to take him to see Santa. Exactly what he needed to help keep his Christmas spirit alive."

"Thank you for coming with us. That really made it special for him."

"Shawn and Alice took him every year. We could have gotten away without doing it, but I'm glad we did."

"Me too."

We stood there, smiling at each other, the silence of the house all around us. She should be going, and I should be heading to my office. Instead, we stood there, staring at each other, a thousand thoughts about how right this felt going through our heads.

I saw her soft smile and the look in her eyes. It looked like love, and I felt like the luckiest guy alive. I wanted that. To hell with fear and those what-ifs. I wanted Hope.

My gaze locked on hers. I lowered my head and captured her lips. Her lips felt soft beneath mine. Soft, willing, wanting. I moved my hands into her hair, holding her so I could caress her lips with mine. Her hair was as soft as silk, and as my fingers got lost in her waves, and my thumb caressed her cheekbones, I knew, deep down, I wanted her to spend the night with me.

"Please stay."

"Stay?"

"Yes."

"As Pete's nanny?" She frowned, pulling away.

I tightened my hold on her, pulling her fully against me so that she felt what she did to me. "And much, much more."

Her gaze softened, and the last of her resistance fell away. Her arms tightened around my neck and she stood on tiptoes to press her lips against mine.

I kissed her back with all the desire I felt for her. I gripped her hips and pulled her tightly against me. She groaned and threw her head back, exposing that sweet spot where her neck met her collarbone. I trailed kisses down her throat, across her shoulders. I lifted my head and held her gaze.

"I want you."

"I want you too."

I walked her backward and then took her hand. I led her down the hall to the guest room. Her eyes widened with surprise.

"I want you in my bed, but I don't want to confuse Peter."

"Okay." She nodded.

I breathed a sigh of relief. I wanted her tonight, and possibly every night, but I didn't want to be thoughtless to her or to Peter. Slowly, because I knew it had been a while for her, and in spite of the desire riding me hard, I unbuttoned her shirt, one button at a time. I pushed it off her shoulders and dropped more kisses on her exposed flesh.

She was as soft as cashmere. I reached behind her and unclasped her bra. I held her gaze, watching for an objection. There was none. She wanted me as badly as I wanted her. Her bra fell away to reveal high, perfect breasts pointed with desire.

I laved her nipple with my tongue. Her fingers dug into my shoulders. Her head fell back. I took my time, licking and suckling her nipple. My cock hardened and pressed painfully against my fly. I unzipped my pants to release the pressure, even as I switched to her other nipple and gave it the same attention. Her hands played in my hair, gripping me tightly, holding me against her breasts, silently urging me not to stop. I didn't need the encouragement. I never wanted to stop.

"Can I have you?"

"Yes," she whimpered.

I unbuttoned her jeans and unzipped them before

touching her over her soft panty. She moaned and withered in my hands. I captured her mouth with mine again even as I caressed her wet mound. She ground her core against my hand, silently asking me to go deeper, giving me permission to explore more of her.

I dipped a finger between her folds and was immediately engulfed in liquid heat.

"God, you're wet. And so fucking tight."

"It's been a while." Her hands trailed down my chest, my stomach, and brushed tentatively against my pulsing cock.

"Yeah?" I asked, feeling a primitive surge of pleasure at her admission. "Squeeze me hard."

She wrapped her hand around my cock and did as I commanded. Her hands were entirely too gentle for my pent-up passion. Gripping her waist, I turned her so that her back was to the bed and gently pushed her down on it, towering over her. I claimed her lips, or she claimed mine. It was a hot, all-consuming kiss as teeth and tongue collided with its match. She moaned in protest when I pulled away. Her hands slipped from around my neck to trail down my chest, curling through the hair on my chest. I pulled her jeans and panty down her legs and free of her feet. Sitting back, I pushed my pants off me as well, then reached into my pocket for my wallet. I took out the condom I always kept in there and tore the packet with my teeth. It had been months since I'd placed it there. God, I hoped it was still good. Quickly, unwilling to wait another minute, I sheathed myself and turned toward her.

She lay there, watching me, waiting for me. She smiled and lifted her arms, encircling my neck, pulling me down on top of her. Her lips met mine again. I sank into her and felt her give way to me. I groaned at the sheer pleasure of being inside her soft warmth. I know it had been months since I'd been in a woman, but had it ever felt this good? Or was it

Hope? I lifted my head and met her eyes. I saw the tears shining there.

"You okay?"

She nodded, resting her palm against my cheek. "Yes."

"Ready?"

She frowned, her eyes narrowing. I slowly thrust into her. She gasped. I thrust again and again, increasing the pace until she was moaning, her nails digging into my back. She moved her hips, meeting me at every thrust. Pleasure raced along my spine. I felt the heaviness in my balls. I was going to come. But not without her.

I grabbed her leg and wrapped it around me. I trailed my hand up the outside of her thigh and then over to that bundle of nerves where we were joined. I strummed them and watched as she tilted her head. She closed her eyes. Her mouth fell open in a silent gasp. I thrust harder, once, twice, and felt her explode around me, clenching me even as she doused me with her liquid heat. I thrust one more time and came inside her, falling over the precipice and landing in a sea of pleasure.

Gradually, our breathing returned to normal. I turned on my side and draped my hand over her waist. I turned her and felt a warmth of satisfaction when she curled into my side, her hand trailing along my chest.

"Are you okay?"

She nodded her head. I hugged her tighter and kissed the top of her head. I could feel sleep coming over me. I hadn't felt this good in months. I closed my eyes and gave myself over to the river of peace flowing over me.

CHAPTER 19

HOPE

What had I done?

I'd just slept with Darius. We'd screwed. Banged. There were no nice words to describe what we had just done. Our sex had been raw, passionate, primitive, and all-consuming. Now he lay next to me, his breathing even, and I felt the burden of our rashness.

What had we done?

I'd been attracted by the look in his eyes, the chemistry in his touch, the passion in his kisses. All of it had been my undoing.

Now what? Where did we go from here?

I looked over at Darius and my heart dropped. He was watching me. I smiled, but he lifted his hand and brushed my hair off my forehead.

"Regrets?" he whispered.

I bit my bottom lip. What could I tell him? The truth. Only always the truth.

"Something in between."

He sighed and pushed himself up on his elbow. Leaning over me, he trailed his fingers across my cheek and over my lips. "You didn't like it?"

"Oh my God, Darius! No. That's not it."

He smiled his cocky smile that did a number on my heartbeat. "Then, what?"

"As great as that was, it complicates everything."

"Does it have to?"

"I can't do causal sex."

"There was nothing causal about that." He smirked. I rolled my eyes, and he quickly laughed. "Wait. That's not what I meant. What I'm trying to say is that was more than a causal hookup. I don't know what it means for us. I don't have a label for it. Look, I get what you're saying. I have the same concerns. I don't want to disappoint you or Peter. But, Hope, this was incredible. I'm very attracted to you, and I know you feel the same way about me. What if we just let this take its course. We're both single adults who enjoyed each other a whole lot. That was as good as paradise, Hope. Why can't we just see where it leads to?"

It had been paradise. Best sex of my life. Even now, my body tingled at the thought of another round with Darius. Did I want to deprive myself? Did I want to resist him? Did I have to?

"Peter?"

"This doesn't have to affect him."

"I don't know. What happens when we don't want to do this anymore?"

"Can we cross that very distant, very far off bridge when we get to it?"

He had a point. I couldn't see myself tiring of Darius. Unless…

"What happens if you meet someone else?"

"You stand a better chance of meeting someone. You're the first woman I've wanted in months. I was single even before the accident. I'm not looking for a relationship or to find someone else. You're the only one I want."

I'd settled into Darius's life without a hiccup. We ate breakfast and dinner together almost every day. I was always at his house, and I was helping him care for his nephew whom he'd taken charge of. I made his life easier, and I honestly didn't mind doing that. But entering into a sexual relationship with him was walking into dangerous territory.

I didn't do casual sex. I needed love and commitment. Wasn't that why I'd walked away from Johnathan? *Good Bones.* Was I settling for less with Darius? He wasn't looking for love, just a warm body in his bed. It was similar to what I'd had with Johnathan and I'd only lasted three months before my desire for more drove me out the door. Was I really thinking about doing this again with Darius?

He dipped his head and touched his lips to mine. The emotion bursting to life inside of me felt like coming home. I wrapped my arms around his neck and pulled him closer. I could kiss him like this every second of every day if it made me feel like I'd come home and all was right with the world.

He trailed kisses down my neckline, over my shoulder blades and across my chest. When he licked my nipple, I felt the flood of desire pool at my core. He suckled on my nipple. I arched my back, pressing myself more fully against him. His tongue worshipped my breast. I never wanted this passion to end.

I parted my legs as he settled between my thighs. There was no rush this time as he entered me. Slowly, he pushed into me until I didn't know where he stopped and I began. He buried his face in the crook of my neck as he moved slowly, exquisitely in me. If we'd fucked before, we were definitely making love now. It was better than before, if that was even possible. As we climbed higher and higher on that emotional scale to a place where we had to claim our release, I felt myself splitting in half and being glued back together again with Darius inside of me.

Shoot! Me and my impulsive decisions.

There was no walking away from this now.

CHAPTER 20

HOPE

The next morning, Darius stayed with Peter so I could run over to my apartment and pack a small bag. It was early still, only six am in the morning when I pulled into my parking spot in front of my apartment. I was climbing out of my car when I noticed the sleek sports car parked across from mine. I stumbled over myself, unable to believe my eyes. On cue, Johnathan opened his car door and stepped out.

Hot blood rushed to my head and pounded in my ears. "Johnathan! What in the hell are you doing here?"

"You're spending the night with him now?"

"I can't believe you."

Had Johnathan spent the night in his car, parked outside my apartment, waiting for me?

My hands and knees trembled as adrenaline coursed through my body. I didn't believe in violence, but I wasn't above defending myself. If he came anywhere near me, I swear I was going to punch him. Turning, I raced up my stairs, anxious to get into my apartment.

"What do you think he wants from you? A guy like that? Do you think he's serious about anything? About you? You're a convenience for him."

I didn't respond. But I felt my own doubt slice through my heart. His words hit close to home. It was what I had thought myself last night as I'd lain next to Darius. It hurt to hear Johnathan put into words what I'd been thinking myself.

"Wise up, Hope!" He grabbed on to my arm as we reached the top of the stairs and swung me around to face him.

"Let go!" I pulled my arm out of his hold. Every muscle in my body went stiff.

Johnathan let go of my arm, throwing both his hands up in the air as he took a step back. "I'm offering you something more. More than you have with him. Why settle?"

I inserted my key in the lock and turned to face Johnathan. "My relationship with Darius is none of your business. Stop following me. Stop waiting outside my apartment for me. You're seriously scaring me now. Is that what you want? Stop it, or I swear, Johnathan, I'm going to the police for a restraining order."

I opened my apartment door and slipped in, shutting it in his face. I flung the deadbolt home and only then did I breathe easily. What in the world was going on with him? His behavior was odd and over the top. He was being wildly persistent, refusing to take no for an answer. I wish he'd paid half this much attention to me when we'd been dating. Perhaps then, I would be willing to give us another chance. As it was, I had no idea why he was suddenly so interested in pursuing me.

I pulled my small suitcase off the shelf in my closet. Hurriedly, I gathered the few items I wanted to take with me to Darius's house. A few sweaters, some jeans, two pretty dresses in case we went to dinner, some lounge wear, and my toiletries.

Johnathan hadn't said anything that I hadn't already been thinking. I wasn't going to let his questioning get the better of me. Yet, it did make me wonder if I was doing the right thing by moving in with Darius.

All right, so it was just temporary and only through the Christmas holiday. After Christmas, I would resume going home in the evenings. Perhaps Peter's long-term nanny would have become available by then.

A pang of loneliness hit me at the idea of not having Peter during the day. I'd always had a special spot in my heart for Lil' Pete. Now that I had grown close to him during these past two weeks, I could safely say that I loved him. I wanted what was right and best for him, of course. But what about me and my heart? Could I take it when his full-time nanny took over and I no longer had to watch him during the day?

What about my desire not to settle for less than a relationship with a good foundation? I knew Darius had it in him to make a woman very happy. He might not believe that about himself, but it was true. Was I looking for him to make me that woman? We hadn't agreed on anything permanent. In fact, all we'd agreed about was the fact that we wanted to keep making love to each other. Platonic was out of the question for us.

Opening my apartment door, I surveyed the parking lot. There was no sign of Johnathan or his car. Breathing easier, I stepped out of my apartment and locked the door behind me before hurrying down to my car. Glancing around, I unlocked my car door and put my bag on the passenger seat. I slid in behind the wheel and started the car. The soothing sounds of *Its Beginning to Look a Lot Like Christmas* floated through my car speakers.

My trembling had stopped by the time I turned onto the street leading into McKnight Grove. I waved to the guard at the security gate and drove into the secluded neighborhood.

Darius opened the front door as I pulled into his courtyard. He was already dressed in his work shirt and trousers. He smiled at me and approached as I shut off the engine and opened my door.

"How'd it go?"

"Pretty good." I bit my tongue to keep from telling him about my weird encounter with Johnathan. I didn't want to slow Darius down, and part of me hoped Johnathan had gotten the message.

"Got everything you needed?"

"Yeah." I let him pull me into his arms and press a kiss on my upturned mouth. Heat unfurled in my stomach and a desire for more burned through me.

This was the difference between Johnathan and Darius. The passion between the two of us was more than I'd experienced with Johnathan. It was alive and demanded more from Darius and I than lukewarm affection.

"Come on. Let's put your bag in the guest room."

I felt a twinge of disappointment at his words, then quickly wondered what was wrong with me. It made sense to stay in the guest room and not in Darius's bedroom. It would be less complicated for Peter if we didn't put our relationship on display for him. I barely understood what our relationship meant and where it was going. I didn't want to do anything that would confuse Peter in the long run.

The three of us ate breakfast together and then Darius left for work. Pete and I did some math together, worked on a puzzle, watched his favorite television show and then I read to him. By the time I put him down for a nap, I felt slightly sleepy myself. Perhaps it had to do with my late-night activities or getting up early to drive over to my apartment. However, as Pete fell asleep, holding my hand, I didn't hesitate to stretch out next to him on his bed and curl up on my side.

I listened to his breathing even out. He was such a wonderful boy. He was everything I wanted in a son. And this moment here was what I dreamed about when I thought of being married and having children. Before anxiety and worry over whether I was settling for less with Darius could overtake me, I reminded myself that there hadn't been any prospects for a relationship before Darius had walked into my classroom and asked me to be Pete's nanny for Christmas. There wasn't anyone that I had been dating and certainly no one I'd set my sights on to have a relationship with. We were only four days till Christmas. Soon, Darius's full-time nanny would start, and I would be left with only memories of caring for Pete. And what about my time with Darius? I didn't know. I gave in to the heaviness demanding that I close my eyes and felt my body go limp with release. It was all worth pondering, but it was best done at another time. I was simply too tired right now to worry about where my relationship with Darius was heading. Or what our current relationship did for my desire to have a lifelong relationship.

CHAPTER 21

HOPE

I held on to Peter's hand as Darius's assistant led the two of us down a long, carpeted hallway toward the conference room where Darius and his partners were working.

My heart felt like a million butterflies were holding on to it as they soared toward the sky. At any second now, I was sure it would leap out of my chest. I was surprised the petite woman in front of me didn't hear it beating.

I regretted the rash decision I'd made this afternoon to visit Darius at his office on our way to the zoo. Pete and I had both woken up from our nap, refreshed and ready for another adventure. After spending most of the day at the house, I'd decided to take him to the zoo to see the animals and then the Christmas lights that came on at dark. Part of me had hoped Darius would accompany Peter and me to the zoo too. But after the lukewarm greeting from Darius's assistant, and the quietness of the office, I realized that he was busy, and I was interrupting him.

His assistant pushed on a frosted glass door and stepped aside so I could walk in holding on to Peter's hand.

"Hey, guys!" Darius pushed his chair away from the large conference table and walked toward us.

I had an impression of lots of light and windows that afforded a view of the sunny, crisp afternoon outside, before Darius was smiling down at me. He swung Peter up into his arms.

"Everything okay?" he whispered.

"Yes. I'm sorry. I should have called first before dropping by. I thought I would take Peter to the zoo."

"That's okay. Sounds like fun. Come, let me introduce you to the guys."

Some of the tension I'd felt since stepping onto his floor eased as he swung an arm around my shoulders and walked me over to the table and the two men in suits standing there.

"Hope, these are my business partners, Brian and Hayden. Guys, you remember Hope?"

"Yes," they both said in unison.

"It's nice to see you again." The blond, brooding giant named Brian smiled at me before reaching over to rub Peter's back.

"Hey, big guy. How are you doing? You've gotten taller since I last saw you."

"No kidding. He's growing like a weed." Hayden came around to stroke Peter's head. Peter rested his head on Darius's shoulder and hugged him tighter.

Hayden was the dark, handsome one. I'd met both men months ago at Shawn and Alice's burial. They'd been silent and sad standing in the background, giving quiet support to Darius.

A moment passed where no one said anything, and I was sure the three men were remembering Peter's father. They'd lost a friend and a business partner. They'd done a great job moving on, but I was sure that me bringing Peter here had to have reminded them of what they'd lost.

This was a mistake. Heat washed over my face and down my neck. I'd created a distraction and thrown them all for a loop.

"You guys look busy. Peter and I should be going."

"I'll walk you out." Darius smiled, but I felt the tension radiating off him.

I waited until we were standing in front of the elevators before apologizing again.

"I really am sorry for dropping by unexpectedly. I can tell I threw you off."

"Only because I find myself wishing I could go with you and Peter."

"You do?"

He nodded. "I love spending time with the two of you, and I want to see his face when he sees the animals and the Christmas lights and decorations at the zoo."

"But you can't?"

He shook his head. "Too much to do. We've got that big dinner meeting next week, and the ground-breaking right after the new year if we can get Kent settled down. The guys and I really need to fine-tune a few of the details."

"Okay. So, you're working late?"

Darius nodded. "We may need to work an extra hour or two. I'll text you."

"Okay. No worries." I smiled, even though anxiety and doubt wrestled with me.

"Be safe," Darius said just as the elevator doors opened. He leaned over and kissed Peter on his cheek, before briefly touching my lips with his.

I held his gaze as the elevator doors closed, sealing him out. I felt guilty that I'd made him feel like he had to choose, and even guiltier that he might be feeling bad for having chosen work over an afternoon at the zoo with us.

I loved spending time with Darius, but it was the middle of the afternoon, and it wasn't logical of me to feel disappointed that he couldn't just take off at the slightest invite. He was running a multi-billion-dollar company, for God's sake. He had a lot on his plate. Yet, disappointment was exactly what I was feeling.

What in the world had prompted me to come down here, unannounced? I hadn't thought to call him. I'd only wanted to see him. Be close to him. I'd been excited about hanging out at the zoo with him and Peter. It hadn't once crossed my mind that he might not be able to join us. Now I felt like an idiot.

I buckled Peter into his car seat and closed the door. I slid behind the wheel of Darius's jeep and took a moment to take a deep breath before I buckled my seatbelt.

I was falling in love with Darius.

Owning the truth, I closed my eyes.

There was no other way to explain why I wanted to be with him so much. My desire to spend time with him and Peter, together, as a unit, was putting me in a compromising situation. Worst, I was making demands on Darius that weren't fair. I knew he cared for me. But was it love? He'd never once indicated that he was in love with me.

I didn't want a causal relationship. I wanted marriage and a family. It was why Johnathan and I had broken up in the first place. But Darius had his hands full with his business and with Peter. He was just beginning to pull things together after Shawn and Alice's death. Was he ready for a committed relationship?

Even though he liked me, and I knew he did, Darius was a

bachelor. Confirmed bachelor. Of his choosing. He had his work and he had Peter. Would he want more? I didn't know. We weren't on the same page when it came to a relationship. And I wasn't sure if I could settle for less. As much as I loved being with him.

CHAPTER 22

DARIUS

"What's going on with you?" Brian whispered.

I lifted my head to find him staring at me across our conference table. I glanced down the length of the table to Hayden who stood at the end, poring over a series of blueprints. He hadn't heard us.

I sighed and ran my fingers through my hair. What could I tell him? The truth? That I'd made love to my nanny, several times, and now I was obsessed with her? Unable to get enough? So much so that I'd move her into my house? Not my bedroom, yet, but certainly we were heading there because how long before I gave in to my desire to see her in my bed and make love to her there?

"Is it Peter?" Brian continued.

I shook my head. For once, it wasn't Peter. "No. Pete's fine."

I was the one that was spiraling out of control. Moving

further away from everything I believed and had decided to work for, and invariably setting myself up for failure.

"I slept with Hope."

"You did?" His eyes bulged and his jaw went slack.

I nodded and glanced at Hayden to make sure he was still preoccupied at the other end of the table.

"Yes."

"And?"

I rubbed the nape of my neck. "And it was great."

"So, what's the problem?"

"It complicates things."

Brian rubbed his chin with his index finger. "Okay. Tell me."

"Hope doesn't do casual sex, and I don't know where I want this to go. Pete loves her. It's going to break his heart if she disappears from his life."

"Yeah, that's tough."

Heat flooded my face. "That's all you have to say?" Brian sounded like I expected Hayden to. Where was his usual intelligent and level-headed advice?

"Right now? Yes. You're overthinking it, Darius. As usual. You're jumping to the end when you're only just getting started. You and Hope are both single, right? Neither one of you sleep around. Your attraction was strong enough for you to get intimate with one another. Why are you assuming it's going to end?"

"Because I'm not looking for a girlfriend, and I know Hope. She's the type of woman who would want something permanent."

"Did she tell you that? Or are you assuming? Maybe what she wants is you. Maybe whatever you have to offer is good enough for her right now."

My mind raced with the possibilities as I considered what he'd said. Could he be right? Hope deserved more, but I didn't know if I could give more. Didn't know if I was capable. There was only one thing I was certain of: I couldn't stomach the thought of another man touching her.

Later that evening, as I drove home, I wondered if I could just let things develop at their own pace? Did I have to put a label or a demand on our relationship? Or could I just enjoy what we had.

The sight of the Maserati Levante in my courtyard had my blood rushing to my head. I pulled hard on my parking brake. Grabbing my messenger bag off the passenger seat, I yanked open my driver side door and stepped out, slamming the door loudly behind me.

What was she doing here?

I opened the door and strode through my home, looking for her. I found her in the living room, standing in front of Hope. Peter was playing with his Legos on the other side of the living room, unaware of the tension radiating off the two women.

"Mother. What are you doing here?"

"Darius, as entertaining as it's been watching you and your girlfriend play house, I need to tell you this simply wouldn't work."

"Not that I care, but what the hell are you talking about?"

"It's in Peter's best interest that I assume responsibility for him now. I've watched you do an ill job of meeting his needs these past months. Now you're shacked up with this woman and have pawned his care off on her. Peter deserves more than what you're providing for him."

"How dare you?" Now I knew where the expression seeing red came from. It was as if all the anger had flown to my eyeballs and it was all I could do not to physically remove my mother from my house.

"You, who pawned Shawn and me off on nanny after nanny and couldn't be bothered to be there for us, are telling me about what a poor job I'm doing with Peter? Get out! Get out of my house, and don't come back."

"As usual, you fail to see reason. You leave me no other choice."

Heat raced through my face at her thinly veiled threat. My heartbeat kicked up a thousand decibels, until I could hear the pounding in my ears.

"Try it, Mother. Do your worse. But rest assured, I will fight you on this."

I saw the flare of surprise in her eyes before she lifted her chin. With a final look down her nose at me, she walked past me and slammed the front door behind her.

Hope stood in front of me, a look of horror on her face. Her cheeks were absent of color. The usual sparkle in her eyes was gone. Peter was watching us closely now even as he drove a toy car back and forth on the Lego bridge he'd built. I took a deep breath. And then another, and another, waiting for the anger to dissipate. But all I wanted to do was smash something.

"Hey, Pete. How are you doing, Bud?" I walked over to him and wasn't surprised when he got to his feet and met me halfway, his arms going up for me to pick him up. I held him close as I turned to face a still silent Hope.

"I'm sorry," she blurted out before I could say anything.

"Why?"

"I answered the door without checking the peephole, and she seemed so polite, I let her in when I shouldn't have."

I sighed in relief, not sure what I had been expecting her to admit, but now feeling myself drawn over to her, to comfort her as well. I pulled her into my arms and hugged her close to me. "It's okay. I should have had her name removed from the visitor's list with security a long time ago. This is not your fault."

"What is she planning to do?"

I shrugged. Who knew? My mother had entirely too much time and money on her hands. I'd seen her upset enough to blacklist a member of her staff after firing her so that no one in our community would hire her again.

There was one thing working in my favor, however, and that was her aversion to scandals. I didn't think she would want a public custody battle for Peter. Especially not one that examined her ability to provide a warm, nurturing environment for him.

Shawn and Alice had asked me to be Peter's guardian in the event of their death. They'd stipulated it in their will. They'd made me trustee over his inheritance. That had to count for something. It was obvious what their intention was. My mother was a fool to think she could go against their final wishes, and I wouldn't challenge her every step of the way. Besides, I had made a promise to them that night I would take care of Peter. I meant to keep that promise.

Hope was still trembling in my arms. Peter had rested his head on my shoulder, and I could tell that he was getting sleepy.

"Come on, how about dinner and a Christmas story before bedtime?" I asked them both.

"Sounds wonderful." Hope sighed and pulled away. I let her go even though I wanted to keep her safely pressed against my side.

Mother had accused us of playing house. The three of us ate dinner together, then I sat in the bathroom as Hope gave Peter his bath and then brushed his teeth. I wondered if she'd been right. It certainly felt like a home. Hope had made it that, right down to the glittering Christmas tree in the foyer decked out with red, green, and gold ornaments. Even now, the three of us felt like a family. We felt permanent.

Is that what I wanted? Something permanent with Hope? I didn't even know how she felt about me. Sure, the sex was great. But was that all it was? Did she want more from me? Did I have more to give her? What about Gemini Inc., and the demands that business always made on me? Would Hope grow to resent that? Would she feel trapped here with Peter while I spent long hours at the office. I frowned at the thought as I realized I didn't want to spend long hours at the office away from Hope and Peter. The thought of working late hours held very little appeal for me.

That was why I'd avoided relationships to begin with. Gemini needed my time and attention if it was going to be all that Brian, Hayden, Shawn, and I had envisioned it to be. I'd never wanted to have to choose between a family and work. Now, without even being married, or in a defined relationship, I felt myself examining the demands of both.

"Everything okay?" Hope asked as we walked arm in arm down the stairs and back into the kitchen.

"Yes."

I helped her wash the dishes and tidy up the kitchen after dinner. The silence carried on between us, and with each passing minute, I could sense her getting more and more anxious.

"How about a Christmas movie?" I asked her after she had folded the towel she'd used to dry the dishes and placed it on the kitchen counter. Her sign that kitchen clean-up was complete.

I saw some of the tension leave her shoulders. "Sure. I'd love that."

I nodded and went to the refrigerator, pulling out the bottle of white wine and then getting two glasses down from the cupboard. We walked into the living room, and I set the wine and glasses down on the tray on the coffee table. I turned on the television and scrolled through to one of the streaming services and clicked on the holiday movies category.

"How about this one?" I asked her, stopping on a thumbnail of a man and woman in an embrace outside of a cabin situated in front of a snowy castle.

Hope stared at me before bursting into laughter. "Really?"

"Yeah. What's wrong with the uh," I read the title of the movie, "*The Prince's Christmas Wish?*"

"Nothing." She shook her head, her eyes wide. "I'm totally here for it."

Smiling, I hit play. I could tell what she was thinking. I poured her a glass of wine and settled back with my own. I would give her a minute before I pulled her onto my lap and kissed her.

"What's so funny?" Hope asked.

"You, thinking I wouldn't enjoy a good romantic movie."

"You said Christmas movie, but I thought for sure you would choose some action thriller set at Christmas time. I misjudged you. I'm sorry." She smiled, sipping from her wineglass.

I set my wineglass down on the tray and leaned back against the couch. Wrapping my arm around her, I pulled her against me and held her there. "You can make it up to me later."

I'd picked the movie to score points with Hope, but I found myself enjoying the story of the prince who'd traveled to America to find his soulmate before Christmas, or face having to marry the spoilt princess his parents had picked out for him.

I kissed her after the prince had gotten his girl while the credits were still rolling. Her body relaxed against mine. I pulled away only long enough to take the wineglass out of her hand and set it down next to mine. I claimed her lips again, reveling in the taste of her.

I kissed Hope because she was warm, and caring, generous, and loving. I kissed her because I liked having her in my house, on my couch, in my arms. In no hurry at all, I trailed kisses down her neck, pushing her sweater off her shoulders to reveal her perfect collarbone. The sigh falling from her lips urged me on. Lifting my head, I pulled the hem of her sweater up over her chest and then her head. Dropping her sweater on the floor, I took in the luscious beauty of her breasts encased in satin.

"You're so beautiful," I whispered to her.

A slow smile curved her lips. She reached behind her and unclasped the hooks on her bra. It fell away, revealing her creamy breasts. I cupped them, loving the feel of them in my palms and captured one of her tight nipples with my mouth. I gently bit the taut nipple, eliciting a moan of pleasure from her. I laved it with my tongue to take the sting away and then repeated the action on the other nipple. I felt the ripples of pleasure flowing through her body.

"I want you." She was breathless. Her hands roamed through my hair and gripped tightly, holding me in place against her chest. She arched her body against mine, and I splayed my hand against her hips, holding her firmly beneath me as I sucked her breasts.

Lifting my head, I gazed into her eyes and was lost, because, in the dim light from the television and the kitchen area, I saw the desire in her eyes. I urged her to lean back. I unbuttoned her jeans, and she lifted her hips for me so I could pull them down her legs and off her feet. Her panties were a tempting satin creation that was smooth to the touch, as I pulled them off.

I studied her naked body lying on the couch before me. Her blackish-brown hair fell in loose waves over her shoulders and down her back. Her breasts rose with every deep breath she took, tempting me to kiss them, suck them, make love to them. Her stomach was flat and soft and I couldn't help dipping my head and licking her belly button. She arched her body upward, and bent her knee so that I settled more fully between her legs. I trailed kisses down her belly until I got to the soft mound of her pussy.

Softly, I lick her there. She moaned and lifted her hips, pushing herself against my mouth, demanding more. I held her hips tightly, holding her in place as I worshiped her bundle of nerves with my tongue.

Her whimpers were like music in the otherwise quiet room. I could sense her desperation for more in the way she clung to my head, holding me tightly to her core. I gave in to her demands and pushed my tongue into her wet pussy. It was pleasure for her and torture for me as my hard cock pressed painfully against the fly of my pants.

Over and over, in and out, I pushed my tongue deeper into her until her moans of pleasure were one continuous sound. I licked at the wetness, and with a few more licks of her creamy core, she came apart below me. I didn't stop my administrations until the last of her orgasm passed and she lied back against the couch, completely spent.

I wiped my mouth on my t-shirt before pulling it over my head and dropping it on the floor next to us. I unzipped my pants and reached for the condom in my wallet before dropping my pants to the floor. My hard cock was anxious to be inside her again.

I climbed on top of her, enjoying the pleasure-laden look in her eyes. Loving the way her eyes went wide and her mouth formed that perfect O as I slid into her wetness. I felt her muscles clench around me and bit my lower lip to contain the shout of pleasure that threatened to escape.

Unable to contain the passion demanding that I move deep and hard in her, I slid my hand beneath and cupped her ass, pulling her deeper into me.

I captured her mouth, kissing her deeply. Like age-old lovers, we moved rhythmically together, pushing and contracting, squeezing and demanding. Our bodies knew this dance and the infinite pleasure that came at the end. It was an intoxicating dance that created pleasure at every touch, every push into her as she contracted around me. Together, we raced to that end, and when we went over into paradise together, I couldn't stop myself from showering her with kisses on her mouth, her neck, her breasts. I wanted to consume every part of her.

We lay pressed against each other on the couch. Our breaths mingled together, first panting and then softening as our heart rates decreased. I shifted my weight so that I was no longer on top of her, but kept my leg over her, anchoring her in place lest she tried to escape.

It was then, as I held her in my arms, cherishing the way she felt, that I realized the truth. I adored Hope, and I never wanted this to end.

CHAPTER 23

HOPE

Making love with Darius was out of this world. It wasn't strictly about the passion the two of us shared. It was also about the moments after, when we cuddled in each other's arms and held each other, listening to each other's heartbeats settle.

The quiet conversations we had while holding each other meant the world to me. It was during those moments that he opened up about Peter, and his partners, Brian and Hayden, and the project they were working on that, though demanding, meant so much to them. It was during those times that I told him about the children I taught, and my excitement about the upcoming new school year, and having Peter in my classroom again.

We had settled into a routine that so closely resembled a couple's. Yet there had been no conversations about what this was between us. We simply enjoyed waking up next to each other, cooking and eating breakfast together, getting

Peter ready for the day and then dinner, when we all ate together again before heading out for a bit of late-night shopping.

With Christmas only two days away, the three of us had been shopping late into the night the past couple of days. It should have been madness going to the mall late at night and darting from store to store, buying Lego sets, trains and all the other toys that caught Peter's eyes, but in actuality, it had been fun. All three of us enjoyed the time we spent together, and being in the thick of the Christmas holiday season kept our spirits high, despite the inherent sadness that Shawn and Alice weren't with us.

My phone rang just as I was putting Peter down for a nap. I glanced at the screen and then immediately swiped to take the call. "Hello, Mom."

"Hi, sweetie! How are you? I haven't heard from you in weeks."

I grimaced at the note of condemnation in her voice. "I'm sorry, Mom. I've been helping a friend the last couple of weeks. I texted you about it, remember?"

"Sure, but it's still nice to hear from you. Anyway, you know why I'm calling you, don't you?"

I paused, and after a long sigh, my mom continued, "Christmas lunch, sweetheart! Your dad and I are expecting you. You are coming, right?"

"Yeah, Mom, about that. Do you mind if I bring Darius and Peter along? They invited me to spend the day with them. And I think it would be great for them to get out of the house on Christmas."

"Of course, sweetie. It'll be great to have a child in the house on Christmas again. I'll bake cookies for dessert."

I ignored my mom's hint that she was pining away for grandbabies. She wasn't consciously telling me to hurry up and get it done, but she was definitely ready to be a cookie-baking grandma.

We spoke about my dad and his health, her circle of friends, and what was new in her life before we said goodbye and ended the call. Immediately, I felt the loneliness creeping in. I wanted to be on the other side of the phone call: a mother speaking with her daughter, inviting her over for Christmas lunch. Instead, I was the single daughter with no real prospects in her life.

Darius.

His face filtered through my mind's eye. Was he a prospect? Or was our entire relationship only temporary? We hadn't talked about it, but I knew the new nanny was expected to begin shortly after the new year. What would that mean for me? And my role in his and Peter's life?

"Everything okay?"

I turned to find Darius standing in the kitchen behind me. "Yeah, that was my mom. She's invited us to come over for Christmas lunch."

He didn't say anything right away, but I could feel his hesitation. "I was hoping we could all spend Christmas together. Here."

A hot wave of pleasure and apprehension collided in my chest. "That sounds wonderful. I would love that, except I kind of promised my mom that we would come. I'm sorry if I overstepped. It's just that I always go home for Christmas lunch, and I thought you and Peter might enjoy coming with me. But look, it's no big deal. We can have breakfast here. I can go to my mom's for lunch, and we can catch up for dinner in the evening." I turned away, unwilling to let him see how the thought of being apart from them on Christmas made me feel.

I felt his arms wrap around my waist and pull me against

his solid chest. His palms pressed into my stomach, and I found his tight hold on me comforting.

"Peter and I would love to come with you to your mom's for lunch."

"Yeah?" I wanted to be sure. I didn't want him thinking that he had to do it.

"I'm sorry. My initial hesitation has more to do with my experiences with family lunches. Although your mom and dad can't be all that bad if they raised an amazing daughter like you. So, yes, Peter and I can't wait to meet your parents."

"Yeah?"

"Yeah." He turned me around so that I was facing him. I wrapped my arms around his neck as he lowered his mouth to touch mine.

I didn't know where we were heading. I didn't have all the answers about our relationship and just where we would end up. I just knew in this moment, as he was kissing me and I felt desire and something else curling in my stomach, I wanted more of whatever this was, for as long as I had it.

I wasn't going to make any demands on Darius. I didn't want to force a label on our time together.

He'd never said he loved me. I wasn't going to ask him to. He'd never said our living arrangement was permanent. I wasn't going to ask him if this was.

I just wanted to take this one moment at a time. To hell with classifications and pressure to neatly wrap everything up. Some things didn't fit in a neat box. I was learning to be okay with that.

CHAPTER 24

DARIUS

I glanced at the clock. Seven-thirty. I'd long since blown past dinner. Glancing at Brian and Hayden sitting across the conference room table from me deep in concentration as they pored over the schematics for Project Resilience, I accepted that the three of us still had a long night in front of us. Christmas Eve or no Christmas Eve.

Peter and Hope were probably finishing up bath time by now, and Hope would be getting ready to read Peter a bedtime story. I'd missed dinner and bath time and was most likely going to miss tucking him in as well. The slight twinge of guilt and disappointment I felt in my chest took me by surprise. When had I grown so fond of my familial duty? Caring for Peter was no longer this difficult task I did in honor of my late brother. It was my pleasure. My purpose.

"You know what, guys?" I stood suddenly. Brian and Hayden both looked up. "I'm sorry. It's Christmas Eve and I need to be home with Peter."

"Seriously, man?" Hayden groaned; his face twisted in annoyance. Brian sat back in his chair, but he remained silent.

"I'll make it up to you after the holidays. It's Peter's first Christmas without Shawn and Alice. I need to be with him now."

Hayden opened his mouth to protest, but Brian cut Hayden off.

"Hey, Darius, of course, whatever you need."

"Oh, I see how this is going to go," Hayden grumbled.

"Shut up, Hayden," Brian murmured, turning his attention back to the paperwork.

I slipped out the door and walked hurriedly toward the elevator. Thirty minutes later, I parked in front of my house. The sight of the blue Levante parked in the courtyard had me rushing out of my car. I opened my front door and was hit by the sound of Peter's crying and Hope's quiet, determined voice. I walked into the living room and stopped short. My mother stood there, facing off with Hope who held a crying Peter in her arms.

"What's going on here?" My voice was firm yet low. Peter stopped crying and twisted in Hope's arms to face me. I walked over to him and Hope and reached for him. He came willingly into my arms. I saw Hope's shoulders relax and heard her sigh of relief.

"Darius, for God's sake! Your nanny refused to let me see Peter. She's acting like I'm a stranger rather than his grandmother."

"Mrs. Peyton stopped by unannounced. Again. I let her in, wanting to be polite because she said she had a gift for Peter. But then she wanted to take Peter out to dinner. I told her it was his bedtime. Then she insisted on putting him down to bed. Peter's tired and cranky, and he prefers it when his bedtime routine isn't broken. I tried to explain this to Mrs. Peyton, but she's not willing to leave."

"It's okay, Hope. Would you please take Peter up for his bath? I'll be along shortly."

"Okay."

I waited until Hope and Peter had left the room before turning to face my mother.

"Really, Darius. Wherever did you find her? She has no training whatsoever."

"What are you playing at?"

"Excuse me?"

"Showing up here unannounced. Again! Causing a disturbance. It's Christmas Eve, for God's sake. Why are you even in town?"

"I fly out to meet your father tomorrow afternoon."

"So, what are you doing here?"

"It's our first Christmas without Shawn. He looks so much like him. I wanted to see him."

A twinge of sympathy fluttered across my chest. "You should have called me first. And you shouldn't have argued with Hope in front of Peter."

"It's selfish of you to keep him from me."

I bit my tongue, trying to maintain silence. There was no argument where Helen Peyton wasn't the victim. It was best to just remain silent.

"I expected you to be here. Good God, it's after seven on Christmas Eve. I didn't think you'd be working late. I thought you'd be here for Peter."

I felt my temper flare at the not-so-subtle dig, but another emotion, one that left a sour taste in my mouth, and an icy cold feeling in my stomach, rushed forward on the heels of annoyance.

"I'm here now, and you've seen him. I think it's best for you to leave."

She grabbed her bag off the couch and left shortly. Breathing deeply to steady myself, I massaged the tightness at the nape of my neck. Slowly, my heartbeat returned to normal. My mother's admonishments repeated in my mind. Was I capable of taking care of Peter? I did work late, often, in fact most nights I was late getting home and that was why Hope staying here was such a plus. Was I being selfish by refusing to let Mother see Peter, or help in any way with his care?

I knew what my reasons were. Mother might want to guilt-trip me, but she hadn't changed. I didn't think that she could do any better of a job with Peter than she had done with Shawn and me. Yet, I found myself questioning my capacity as well. That was the part that hurt the most. The fact that I couldn't say that I wasn't doing Peter a disservice by keeping him to myself.

Peter and Hope were upstairs lying on his bed when I walked in. Freshly showered, his hair towel-dried, he looked peaceful snuggled next to Hope as she read him his favorite bedtime story. I leaned against the bedroom door, watching them, listening to them, and feeling confidence in what I was providing for Peter grow once again.

Hope.

It was what I felt watching his heavy eyelids flutter and close over his eyes before his head bobbed down to the pillow. Hope for Peter and for me. Maybe I could provide Peter with the life he deserved. Maybe Hope was the one to help us do it.

"Hi," I whispered to her as we walked out of Peter's room, hand in hand.

"I'm sorry about your mother."

"I should be the one to apologize. I'm sorry you had to deal with her alone."

"I know you wouldn't have wanted her to take Peter out of the house."

"Peter barely knows her. If she cared enough, she would realize that and she never would have pushed you to let him leave with her. Thank you for standing up to her."

"You don't have to thank me for doing that."

She was wrong. I did have to thank her. Not everyone would've gone up against my mother. Hope was an amazing woman and Peter was lucky to have her in his life. What would happen though, when January came around and she went back to her classroom? When she was no longer staying with us? How would Peter react to her disappearance from our home? Was I setting him up to experience another heartache when the holiday was over and Hope returned to teaching full-time?

What about me? Was I in for heartache when she moved out and resumed her life? What could I possibly offer a woman like Hope? Someone who was so obviously created to be a mom and a wife, a nurturer, and a caretaker. Someone whose dream was to be those things. What did I have going for me that I could possibly provide for her?

It would be one thing if she wanted my money or was even remotely attracted to me for what I could physically provide. The truth was that Hope wasn't moved by my wealth. She loved what she did, and she was happy with what she made.

"What are you thinking about?" she asked softly, her face upturned to mine, her arms wrapped around my waist.

I smiled. "How lucky Pete is to have you in his life."

"Oh." She lifted her arms around my neck and pulled me toward her. I gave her my lips and felt the instant rush of arousal.

She ended our kiss far too soon. Her eyes were bright in the dim light. Her cheeks flushed a pretty pink. "And what about you, Mr. Peyton? Are you lucky to have me in your life?" she teased.

I captured her lips again and showed her better than I could tell her just how much she meant to me. Holding her by the waist, I walked her backward toward my bedroom door. Without breaking our kiss, I turned the doorknob and walked us both into my bedroom before closing the door behind us and locking the door.

I was the luckiest man in the world to have her here with me now, and I wanted more. I wanted her in my bed, her head on my pillow. I wanted to know what it would be like to have her body thrashing against my sheets.

My desire clashed with my fear that I was fucking everything up. In the end, desire won as Hope lifted her arms and I peeled her sweater off. Her bra was black satin against her creamy skin, and I stared for a moment, mesmerized with her breasts and how beautiful they were.

I wasn't husband material, but if I were, Hope would be what I wanted in a partner. She was beautiful inside and out. She was heat wrapped up in a delicious package. A temptress and a caretaker. Perfect in every way. There was no way this would last. Chances were I was fucking it up real good. But as I slipped into her velvety warmth and felt her contract around me, I knew I didn't care. I wasn't husband material, but if I were, Hope would be my wife.

CHAPTER 25

DARIUS

"You okay?" Hope whispered in my ear for the hundredth time that day.

It was Christmas Day, and we were standing in her parents' living room, next to their Christmas tree, while Pete was busy ripping open the big box Hope's mom had just handed him.

I nodded, smiled, and sipped on my eggnog. Truthfully, I wasn't okay. I felt hot and it wasn't because of the temperature in the house. My stomach had been churning for the past twenty minutes, and I couldn't get rid of the tightening in my chest, no matter how many deep breaths I took. I was doing my best to keep my overwhelming sense of anxiety under wraps, but Hope's question let me know I was failing miserably.

We'd come over a couple hours ago to have lunch with her mom and dad. It had been a unique experience filled with boisterous conversations and lots of giving. It was just as I had thought. Someone as loving and giving as Hope had to have great parents. Hope's mom had fallen in love with Peter immediately.

I had expected stilted conversations and judgmental glances. Instead, I got open acceptance and quiet approval as Hope's dad engaged me in conversational topics that at times felt like a job interview.

Lorenzo Martinez was an ex-oilman who'd worked in the refineries. He was quiet and preferred to listen to Hope and her mother go back and forth in conversation than to add his two cents. But it was obvious he was involved in his daughter's life and wanted the best for her. At first, I thought he wasn't too sure I was the best for her, but he saw how much Peter and I made Hope happy, so he was willing to suspend judgment. Now, after sitting through a meal with him and answering his questions about my business, Peter, my relationship with Hope and my plans for my future, I felt like I'd passed some unspoken test and I was okay in his books.

While he'd begun to slowly warm toward me, I had begun to feel overwhelmed by the attention and the general coziness of the family. I wasn't accustomed to friendly, talkative family lunches. We were accustomed to quiet affairs, waiting for the meal to be over or the next grenade in the form of a well-formulated question to be launched.

It was too easy sitting around the table on Christmas morning, watching my nephew interact with my lover's family. It called to me in a way that nothing ever had before. Not a deal at work, or anything else that used to hold my attention. Certainly no one else had made me want to be so wrapped up in a relationship with them. What were we doing? We were likely to hurt each other.

"Can I get you a drink?" Lorenzo asked from his position in his recliner across from me.

We were all sitting in the living room watching Peter play

with his new Lego set, his Christmas gift from Hope's parents.

"Would you like a cup of coffee?" Hope chimed in from her seat next to her mom on the sofa.

"No, thank you. I'm full."

"Dad, what about you?"

Lorenzo shook his head and held up the half-full glass of beer he'd been nursing since after lunch.

"Looks like you picked the right one, Beth." Lorenzo nodded at Pete and his Lego set.

"I had a little help from Hope. We're glad he likes it." She directed this last bit at me.

"Thank you both for getting it for him. You didn't have to do that. Thank you for having us over for Christmas too. It's been a wonderful day."

"Well, when Hope told us about you two, we were super excited to meet you. You're the first Hope's brought home for Christmas dinner."

"TMI, Mom."

I laughed, though, the icy tentacles of fear crawled up my spine and wrapped around my neck. Sweat beaded my brow. I wanted to blame it on the fire in the corner, but I wasn't that delusional.

"Well, it's true," her mom continued, oblivious to my growing discomfort.

Stealing a glance at Hope, I noticed the color in her cheeks. She would have preferred that her mother hadn't remarked on the fact that she'd brought Peter and I over for Christmas lunch but had never done that with another man.

Why had she introduced us to her parents? I knew it was because I'd invited her to spend the day with Peter and me and she hadn't wanted to break her family tradition. Was it also because she hadn't wanted to be away from me? From

Peter? Could it be that she felt more for Peter and me than she'd let on?

What was I doing? Was I stringing Hope along? Standing in the way of her pursuing a relationship with someone else? Her ex, maybe?

I was selfish enough to like the fact that no other man had experienced the privilege of Christmas lunch with Hope and her parents. But I felt the massive weight of guilt tugging at my conscience. It was an anvil around my neck. I was setting Hope up to be hurt.

This was a first for me. I had no experience with happy families and juggling the responsibilities of a relationship with the demands of a career. Did I want to try figuring all of that out with Hope? Didn't she deserve better? Didn't Peter?

Hope was everything a man could hope for. I wanted to relax in the moment and enjoy it, knowing that I was that man here to stay. Even though all I felt was an overwhelming unease and the sinking feeling of impending doom. As good as this was, I just knew that I was going to blow it. Big time.

We drove home in silence. Peter was asleep in the backseat. Occasionally, Hope and I exchanged glances with a smile. My heart raced quickly in my chest. My palms were sweaty. I wanted to blame it on the heat in the car, rather than the beautiful, silent woman sitting next to me. But I knew the truth.

Our relationship scared me. It stirred feelings in me that I'd never experienced before. Worse, it teased me with possibilities of something more, even as I feared that I could never earn it, have it, keep it.

I wished I could talk to Shawn. He would cuff me on my shoulder and tell me to take a breath. Relax and stop overanalyzing everything. He would tell me how out of his element he'd felt when he first met Alice, but then tell me it had all worked out in the end. He would swing his arm around my shoulder and assure me it was all going to be okay. Today, more than anything else, I really wanted to hear him tell me that.

We pulled into my garage. I unbuckled Peter and gathered him into my arms. He was getting bigger. It still warmed my heart when I pulled his body against mine and rubbed my chin in his dark hair. Hope went ahead of me and opened the door leading into the kitchen. I followed her up the stairs and into Peter's bedroom. Together we silently changed him into his pajamas, without waking him up. Pulling the covers up to his chin, we both kissed him on his forehead and waited until we were sure that he'd settled into a deep sleep before leaving his room, pulling the door closed behind him.

"Today was wonderful," Hope murmured, walking ahead of me toward the stairs.

"It was."

I reached for her hand, causing her to stop. We were standing at the top of the stairs. The mammoth pine shone in the foyer; its Christmas lights twinkling, glowing, filling the room with warmth. The garlands running along the banister flashed in a steady rhythm, casting a warm glow along the staircase.

"My best Christmas ever," she whispered.

I smiled at her, pulling her against me. I pressed my lips against hers and kissed her the way I'd wanted to all day. Kissing Hope was easy and felt so right. It washed away the doubts that had been plaguing me all day.

"Mine too."

She beamed at me.

"It's not over yet."

"What did you have in mind?"

I kissed that sweet spot where her neck gave way to her shoulders and felt her answering shiver. Capturing her lips again, I kissed her with an urgency that was driven by the sudden fear creeping along my spine. Hope was as good as it was going to get for me. But what did I have to offer her? And how soon before Hope wanted more? How soon before she decided that she could find it elsewhere? What would it mean for Peter and me? As sweet as Hope was, as patient and as kind, I knew the truth. I wasn't enough for her. It was only a matter of time before she realized that, and all the late nights, the demands of Gemini and raising a child that wasn't hers got to be too much. It was only a matter of time until I lost her.

Not tonight, though. Tonight, she was mine. And as I filled her, taking her higher and higher toward that peak that she loved so much, and I heard her breathless, satisfied moans in my ears, I felt my heart expand in my chest. Tonight, I was all hers, and I was enough.

CHAPTER 26

HOPE

Christmas Day had been one for my record books. I got a glimpse of what it would be like to have my husband and child over to my parents for Christmas lunch. I very much wanted to be there already. The time spent at my mom's reminded me of what I wanted for my life. It made me realize that I was settling.

I'd been attracted to Darius from the beginning. He was handsome, funny, down to Earth, and kind. He was caring, terrific between the sheets, and thoughtful outside of bed. He was a catch! But I didn't know where we were going with this.

I had broken up with Johnathan, determined to hold out for the love that would last a lifetime. Three months later and I was lonely enough to jump into bed with a man who didn't necessarily want the same things that I did. Darius was all about his company's goals and Peter. Perhaps I fit in somewhere in his life. I didn't know. I didn't want to settle, however. *Good bones.* I was holding out for a relationship with a strong foundation. Nothing else would do.

Yet, I loved being with Darius and Peter. We felt like a family. It would be so easy to settle for what we had: easy, uncommitted lovemaking while we cared for a child that we both loved. It could possibly work for a while. But how long before I started to feel like I had settled? Would I hate Darius then? Feeling as if he had chosen his work over me? Would I feel like I hadn't mattered enough to him for him to make the ultimate commitment to me? Would I grow resentful? These were all damn good questions, none of which I had answers for.

The night of Darius's dinner party at his house came upon us like a huge squall. I spent the day entertaining Peter with his new Lego sets while the chef and his assistants set up in the kitchen. I heard their progress, and soon mouth-watering scents wafted through the air.

Darius had asked me to join him and his two business partners to dinner, along with Peter and the important guest they were hoping to impress. I'd agreed, though, I felt odd about the arrangement. Was I attending as an intimate friend of Darius's, as Peter's nanny, or as both? We needed to talk. Clear the air about what we were to each other, and what our expectations should be. I had told myself I would just accept being intimate with Darius and stop wanting the white dress and commitment. But I'd lied to myself because I quickly realized it was impossible to stay with him every night and not want more. Not when I saw how good we were together.

Later that night, we all gathered around the dining table. Darius's business partners were courteous. Though they were opposites of what I expected. Brian seemed the more responsible of the two. He was quiet, reserved. I recognized that he was a thinker. Hayden seemed younger and brasher. He was very handsome, and he knew it. He wore cockiness like a suit, but something told me that his demeanor was all an act, and he wasn't really as brash or cocky as he seemed to be.

Darius's guest of honor was a man in his late fifties. He looked like money and power, but he also had kind, no-nonsense eyes. He deferred to his wife, who had accompanied him, and was as comfortable discussing Santa with Peter as he was asking the three principals of Gemini about the details of the project they were working on together.

We were halfway through dinner when I noticed Peter couldn't stop itching the side of his mouth. He kept bringing his hands to his face, itching at his mouth, and then taking a bite of his food.

"Are you okay?"

"It itches."

"Let me see."

I cupped his cheek in my hand and turned his face toward me. I moved his hand out of the way so I could see his face and gasped. His mouth was swollen, red, and blistered. Tears sprung to his eyes, and he tried once more to itch the spot that was so obviously irritated.

"What's wrong?"

"I think Pete's having an allergic reaction to the food."

Darius was on his feet and walking around the table to where Pete and I sat. He crouched down at Peter's side and studied his swollen mouth.

"The swelling's getting worse."

"I think we should take him to the ER."

"Yes." Darius swung Peter up into his arms as I stood. He seemed to remember that he had a dining room full of guests at that moment. I felt his hesitation, his uncertainty.

"Go, it's okay. Hayden and I will take care of things here," Brian spoke.

"Thank you. I'm sorry, Allen."

"Don't apologize. Mary and I have raised four children. We certainly understand about emergencies."

We strapped Peter into Darius's jeep and I climbed into the back seat with him. Darius drove down his driveway, turning toward the main roadway which led out of McKnight Grove. He was silent as he gripped the steering wheel.

"It's going to be okay," I whispered to both Peter and Darius.

I wrapped my arm around Peter's shoulder and hugged him as best I could around the car seat. He wasn't crying, but I could see the tears in his eyes. Every so often, he lifted his hand to his mouth and scratched at his lips. I held his hand in mine, hoping to deter him from breaking his already raw skin.

We made it to the closest twenty-four-hour emergency center in record speed. Soon, we were in a small exam room, Peter on the big white reclining seat, and the nurse was taking his vitals. When it was all over, they'd determined that he had an allergic reaction to the shellfish in the rice we'd eaten. They gave him a shot and an ointment for the angry rash on his mouth and sent us home with instructions to see his primary care physician within the next couple days for a follow-up.

"That was scary," I commented as I sat quietly in the front seat of the jeep next to Darius. "I had no idea he was allergic." I glanced at the back seat. Peter was asleep in his car seat, the medicine finally kicking in.

"Neither did I. It must be new." Darius sighed. He hung his head, massaging the nape of his neck with his large palm. "I've never been more afraid in my life."

"You handled it well."

"Did I?" He shook his head. "I'm not sure I can do this."

I glanced at Darius, saw the grim set of his face, the thin

line of his lips. He looked at me as the light from oncoming traffic highlighted his face, revealing the shell-shocked look of panic in his eyes.

"Hey, it's okay. Peter is fine. It's okay."

"It's been months since I was in a hospital. I knew Peter wasn't in mortal danger, but at the same time, the fear and anxiety of having him there...I don't know if I'm cut out for this."

"All parents feel this way, Darius. You showed up for Peter. You were there for him. That's all that matters. He's a healthy, adventurous boy. I can't say this will be the last time you're in the ER with him. I pray you never are again. But you were with him, and for Peter, that's what matters the most. You're a great dad. You're more than equipped for this." I reached across the console and took his hand. I squeezed his fingers, hoping to reassure him.

I wasn't sure if Darius heard me or believed what I was saying. Allen Kent and his wife had left by the time we got back. Brian and Hayden sat in the living room while the catering crew cleaned and packed away. They both got to their feet as we walked into the living room. Darius carried a drowsy Peter in his arms.

"Hey, how's he doing?" Brian asked, coming around to Darius to brush his hand over Peter's head.

"It was an allergic reaction. Must have been the shellfish in the rice. He's going to be okay."

"Let me take him up to bed," I offered, reaching for Peter. Darius made the handoff smoothly. I could feel their gazes on my back as I carried him out of the living room.

I hoped Brian and Hayden could help reassure Darius. I had tried, but I suspected he still felt that he was not doing a good job somehow because Peter had ended up in the ER tonight. There'd been no way of knowing about Peter's new allergy. It was like the scrambled eggs all over again. Peter hadn't come with a manual. Darius had to figure this out as he went. He needed to give himself patience to get there.

I changed Peter's clothes and tucked him in. Then I walked over to the wingback chair next to Peter's bedroom window and sat down. Leaning my head against the back of the chair, I listened to his quiet breathing.

Perhaps I needed to cut Darius some slack too where our relationship was concerned. We didn't know where this was heading, and we both needed time to figure it out.

CHAPTER 27

DARIUS

"You okay?"

I sighed at Hayden's question and sank into the sofa. Burying my head in my hands, I took a couple deep breaths.

"That was too close to three months ago."

Both men remained silent, waiting for me to catch my bearings. They remembered how we had rushed to the hospital, only to learn that Shawn and Alice had passed away.

"It was only an allergic reaction, most likely to the shrimp in the rice." I spoke the doctor's prognosis out loud, wanting to remind myself that it was okay. Peter was okay. "What did Kent say?"

Brian and Hayden exchanged a glance. Brian sat in the sofa-chair across from my couch. "He was very understanding. He appreciated the responsible way you handled tonight's emergency. I think it went a long way to reassure him that we're not fly-by-night idiots pulling together one of the biggest deals of his lifetime."

"You and Hope both handled it well. If I didn't know better, I would think there was something more than Peter between you too," Hayden chimed in.

I looked at Hayden and saw his smug smile. I didn't glance at Brian. I knew he hadn't shared anything I'd confided to him with Hayden. Most likely Hayden was throwing out a net to see if he caught a fish. Hope and I had worked as a team tonight to get Peter the medical attention he needed. We had stood together at Peter's bedside, and he'd been reassured by both of our presence.

How would I have handled it if Hope hadn't been with me tonight? Who would I have leaned on? Trying not to have a meltdown as I took Peter to the hospital. I never wanted to be a father and I certainly hadn't wanted to be a single dad. Now here I was, for all intents and purposes.

What would happen when Hope went back to her classroom? I didn't want to think about what it would mean for our romantic relationship, but I did need to start thinking about Peter and his care. Hope had agreed to be his nanny through to the end of the holiday season. I'd gotten comfortable having her care for Peter, but it wasn't a long-term solution. Hope had a life of her own. I wasn't sure where Peter and I fit into it long term. I didn't have the confidence to ask lest I didn't like her answer.

I needed to circle back with the agency to see if a nanny had become available. And I probably needed to speak to someone like Peter's counselor about my doubt of what I was doing. And if I was being honest, I needed to figure out what I felt for Hope, outside of our arrangement with Peter.

The next day, I was sitting at my office desk when there was a rapid knock on my door. I looked up just as my mother pushed past my new assistant who'd been about to announce her presence and walked into my office like she owned it.

I saw my poor assistant's face and reassured her. "It's okay."

She nodded, smiled briefly before pulling the door closed, leaving my mother and I standing there, staring at each other.

"Mother, to what do I owe this special surprise?"

"How are you and Peter doing?"

"We're both fine. But I can't believe you're here to inquire after us. What do you want?"

She set her bag down on the chair closest to her. She folded her hands primly in front of her and proceeded to glare at me. It was her disapproving stare. The one she used when she wanted me to know that she wasn't at all pleased with my behavior. The problem was that I had long since stopped caring.

"Please stop glowering at me. Just spill it and be done. I'm in the middle of something."

"I've asked you to reconsider what's best for Peter, but you've ignored my calls and repeated requests that you enroll Peter at The Kingsley Academy for Boys."

"Oh, for God's sake. Not this again. I'm not sending Peter to a boarding school."

"Soon, the decision will no longer be yours to make." She reached into her zippered bag and pulled out a manila envelope. She held it out for me.

My insides ran cold as I stared at the envelope in her outstretched hand. I balled my hands into fists to stop myself from grabbing the paper and ripping it to shreds in front of her face. Taking a deep breath, I fought for calm.

"What's this?" I asked her.

"I wanted to give you the courtesy of handing you this

myself. It's a legal document I had the lawyers draw up. It gives me guardianship over Peter. Sign it."

"Have you lost your mind?" I asked her calmly.

"Darius, you and I both know that raising a young boy is the last thing you want. Especially as you're building Gemini. Peter deserves more than you and that nanny of yours can provide him. Don't let your pride stop you from doing what's right."

"It's not my pride, Mother. I'm surprised you would think that I was holding on to Peter because, what? I don't want to admit defeat?"

I snorted in disgust. "That's the type of crap you or Father would do. I took Peter because Shawn and Alice asked me to in their will. But I love Peter. He's mine. I'm not turning his care over to anyone. Especially you and father. So, you can make a mess of him the way you did Shawn and me."

"A mess?" she sputtered. "You boys had the finest care, the best schools -"

"And not much else!"

"You're still blaming your father and me for your inability to form relationships."

"No, Mother. I'm blaming you and Father for being neglectful parents who were too busy with work and your social obligations to give a damn about your children. I'm not about to let you do the same thing to Peter just so you could put a checkmark in some box on a long list you've got going."

"What you think is irrelevant. I will take you to court if I must. I don't think you want the negative publicity for Gemini."

"And what about Father? Do you think he wants the negative publicity?"

Her eyes narrowed, and I continued, "I will go to every news outlet in the country and tell them all about your loving relationship with your husband. I will lay all your shit bare. By the time I'm finished, no one would ever consider you two fit to raise a child. What would that do to your reputation?"

"You wouldn't dare."

"I would! If it meant saving Peter from your idea of a 'childhood.' It's insane the way you and Father shipped us off."

"It was what was expected. Do you think that you just happened to grow into your role here at Gemini Inc.? You were groomed and shaped to be the CEO you are today. That's what I'm trying to offer Peter: a chance to step into his father's legacy someday."

"Shawn would not want Peter in a boarding school. Shawn and I had each other and it was still unbearable. I know for a fact, Shawn would object to what you're proposing. And, Mother, even if he didn't, I do. And I'm Pete's guardian."

"For how long?" I frowned, and she continued, "How long before you decide you could be doing something other than tending to a four-year-old boy."

"I'm not you or Father. I would never abandon Peter."

Her smile was a smirk. It jabbed under my skin.

"I don't have to convince you. But you do need to get out of my office. Now. And take your papers with you. I'm not signing anything. And I am prepared to fight you for him."

"You've always been an impulsive fool. Save your fight, Darius. You're going to need it if think you can raise Peter on your own without my help." She picked up her handbag and walked out of my office.

I stood in front of my desk, long after she was gone, not moving, and wondering if she was right.

I wanted to raise Peter myself. I wanted a relationship with Hope. But the demands of my business hadn't changed.

I'd seen firsthand how Shawn and Alice had fought to keep their relationship front and center in the midst of all the demands on their time. Would they have succeeded if that drunken driver hadn't crossed lanes?

Would I succeed? Or would I only end up hurting Peter and disappointing Hope?

CHAPTER 28

HOPE

I was sitting in a chair in Peter's bedroom watching him play with his Legos when my phone rang. Glancing at the screen, I felt a burst of irritation in the pit of my stomach. Johnathan. I silenced the chiming cellphone and turned my attention back to Peter.

I hadn't spoken to Johnathan since I'd threatened him with a restraining order. He hadn't called me, and since I hadn't been back to my apartment, I hadn't seen him either. Why was he being so persistent? I couldn't believe or understand his actions. We'd been comfortable together, but it hadn't been unchartered passion or desire. It hadn't been anything to write home about. In fact, I knew Johnathan had been only mildly interested. His job and his boss's daughter had suddenly taken up more real estate in his thoughts than I had. So, why he was still pursuing me? I had no idea. Maybe it was because he didn't like losing?

My phone chimed with an incoming text. I picked it up

even though I suspected that it was him again. The image on the screen felt like I'd stepped into air when there should have been solid ground. A picture of Darius and a young blonde sitting at a table in a restaurant glared at me on the screen. He was dressed in his business suit, but his tie was missing. She looked young, in her early twenties, her hair pulled back into a ponytail, wearing a crisp blue shirt and jeans.

For a moment, everything stood still, and I couldn't move. The sounds in the room receded to silence as I stared at the image, unable to look away from Darius's smiling face as he leaned forward in his chair listening to whatever the woman was saying.

Another text from Johnathan popped up on my screen.

You're a joke, Hope. While you're home watching his kid, he's out with another woman.

I lowered my phone to my lap and shook my head to clear the sudden dizziness I felt. Swallowing past the tightness in my throat, I blinked, focusing on the little boy still playing, unaware that my world had cracked clear down the middle. I took a deep breath, willing myself to calm down. A strong sense of betrayal battered my mind. Pinching my lips together, I blinked away the tears threatening to escape. Lifting my chin, I got off the floor and went over to Peter.

"Hey, sweetie. Let's move this game downstairs to the living room, okay?"

He nodded, and I helped him pick up the Lego pieces and place them in his plastic bin. Then I carried it down the stairs. After I'd set him up in the living room, I went into the kitchen. It was only a little before one in the afternoon. I still had six hours before Darius came home. Should I call him now? No. I wanted to see his eyes when I asked him who the girl was.

I don't know what Johnathan thought to gain by pointing

out that Darius was seeing someone else. More proof that Johnathan wasn't in tune with my emotions and what was important to me. If he was, he wouldn't have been so hurtful in the way he'd told me that I'd essentially made the same mistake again. Fallen for a guy who didn't know how to be faithful.

I busied myself in the kitchen washing up the lunch dishes, then figuring out what I was doing for dinner. I checked on Peter and sat with him in his bedroom again while he lied down for a nap. I was functioning on autopilot. Outwardly, I was as calm as a lake's surface. Beneath the surface? I felt like a whirlpool. My emotions were everywhere. My thoughts were unruly and scattered. I wavered between wanting to call Darius now and deciding to wait until he got home. I couldn't decide if I ought to confront him at the front door or pretend that I didn't know anything.

I was a hot mess, and I hated being this way. Suddenly, I knew. I couldn't make believe with Darius anymore and pretend that this - what we had - was enough. It was why I'd walked away from Johnathan. How much more of a hypocrite or a fool would I be if I stayed in a relationship that was good but didn't scratch the surface of what I hoped for? Darius was everything I wanted in a husband. Peter was everything I wanted in a son. Living with them, taking care of them, it was everything. I wanted the good bones. I'd thought I could settle for the little I had now with Darius, but I was wrong. It was wonderful, but it was only a piece of the bone. I wanted the entire thing: good bones, strong foundation. I couldn't settle. It was the promise I'd made to myself while watching Alice and Shawn that night. It was a promise worth keeping.

Where would that leave Darius and me? My stomach turned over and sunk like a rock thrown into choppy waves. The feeling of absolute loss was astonishing. I wanted to believe there would be another outcome, but reality would not let me. Darius enjoyed being with me, but he didn't love me. He didn't crave a future with me. He didn't feel for me what I felt for him. Ultimately, he would walk away because we wanted different things for our future. The fissure in my heart cracked wide open and I felt the tears on my cheeks that came with the loss. There was no denying it. Darius and I were over because the minute I asked for more and he had none to give, I would have to walk away.

CHAPTER 29

HOPE

*L*ater that day, I looked up from Peter's coloring book as Darius walked into the kitchen, followed closely by the same woman in the photograph Johnathan had sent to me. My stomach somersaulted as if I'd just gone over a bend on a rollercoaster. I met his gaze across the kitchen space and saw the same causal smile that curved his lips and made him look like an older yet still adorable version of Peter. I straightened, setting my crayon down.

"Hey, guys. I brought a friend over for dinner."

I didn't say anything. I saw Darius's frown before he set his messenger bag down on the table. "Pete, come here a second, will you?"

Peter climbed off the stool in front of the kitchen bar where we'd been coloring and rushed over to Darius and the young girl who stood at his side, a smile on her face.

"Peter, this is Gwen."

Gwen crouched down on Peter's level and held out her

hand for him. Peter hesitated, then he placed his hand in hers.

"Peter, it's nice to meet you. Your uncle Darius told me all about you. Looks like you were busy over there."

Peter nodded. "I'm coloring with Miss Martinez."

Gwen's gaze met mine, then she smiled down at Peter again. "I heard you've got a great Lego collection. Your uncle mentioned you like to build things. Why don't you show me what you've been doing while Miss Martinez and your uncle get dinner ready?"

I waited until Gwen and Peter had collected his coloring book and left the room before I met Darius's eyes again. He was looking at me silently. He'd rolled his shirtsleeves up around his elbows, and his hands were clasped in front of him.

"What's going on?"

He sighed, then took a step toward me. "I'm sorry. I should have called you and given you a heads-up."

I frowned. It wasn't what I'd been expecting.

"Who is she?"

"Gwen's the nanny the agency found for us."

"The nanny?"

"Yes. They called me back earlier today. Gwen had availability to start immediately. We had lunch together and I think she'll be a great fit for Peter. I invited her to come over this evening so the two of them could spend some time together, getting familiar with each other."

"Why didn't you call me?"

His gaze drifted away before finding mine again. "Please don't make a big deal about it. It happened suddenly. I didn't expect the agency to call me back this week. But, maybe it's for the best?"

"The best?"

"Yeah, Peter can start getting used to someone else. You have your life to get back to, right?"

Disbelief had a laugh escaping my lips before I could stop myself. "My life? Right." I smiled even though it felt like my world was collapsing. I'd been a fool, making long-term plans that included Darius and Peter, while he had no interest in a permanent situation with me.

"I mean, that's been the goal all along, right?"

I nodded. "So, what happens now?" I asked him, leaning against the counter. I couldn't meet his gaze. It was okay because he wasn't meeting mine either.

"If Peter likes her, she can start full-time tomorrow. I hope you wouldn't mind helping her with the transition. She and Peter hit it off well, and he seems like he'll be comfortable with her, but..." He shrugged, rubbing the nape of his neck before shoving his hands into his pants pocket.

"Darius, it's okay. I'm happy to help," I reassured him.

I smiled, but on the inside, my heart was breaking. I needed to go. I was in over my head, drowning. How had I gotten here? I'd thought for sure Darius and I were heading toward something more meaningful than friends with benefits. The joke was on me.

"Thank you, Hope." He hesitated a moment, then said softly, "I'm sorry."

There it was, finally. The apology I deserved for being blindsided. Hot tears stung my eyes. I shook my head and turned away. I wasn't going to cry in front of him. I'd made a mistake. That was clear, but at least, it could have been worst. I could have done something utterly stupid like telling him I loved him and wanting to be with him. Admitting my feelings for him would have left me devastated when he didn't reciprocate. At least now, we both had an excuse for a graceful exit.

Gwen needed to move into my bedroom, and though I

was spending more time in Darius's master suite, neither of us was ready for Peter to discover that. So, it made sense that I would move back to my apartment, and Gwen would occupy the space that I had moved into.

Her presence effectively ended my budding relationship with Darius. I wondered if he realized that. Was it what he wanted? Did he suddenly have the out he'd been wanting?

"No worries, Darius. It's okay."

He turned and walked out of the kitchen, leaving me standing there, alone in my heartbreak.

CHAPTER 30

HOPE

The ringing telephone jolted me out of my thoughts. I glanced around the room until I spotted the phone on the console. Gwen and I glanced at each other. I waved my hand, encouraging her to continue her play with Peter. This was the first time I'd heard the landline ring since I'd started watching Peter. Jumping to my feet, I walked over to the phone and picked up the receiver.

"Good afternoon, may I speak with Darius Peyton?"

"He's not available now. May I take a message?"

"Yes. Please let him know that the Kingsley Academy for Boys called regarding his application. Would you please ask him to return the call?"

"Yes, of course."

I put the receiver back in the cradle, barely mindful of what I was doing. The sound of the woman's voice on the other end of the line felt like an electric shock straight to my heart. The Kingsley Academy for Boys was the prestigious boarding school that Darius's mother had wanted Peter to be enrolled in. Had Darius listened to her and relented about putting Peter in boarding school? When had he applied?

I turned to stare at the little boy playing with Gwen in the middle of the carpeted living room floor. Boarding school? Was that what was best for him? I didn't think so. Yet Darius hadn't mentioned this to me. Just as he hadn't mentioned that Gwen was going to be starting soon.

What was I doing? I'd molded my life to fit Darius's needs and had given myself over totally to caring for Peter. It was supposed to be temporary, just through the end of the holidays and the start of the school season. I'd fallen hard for the both of them, though. Now it seemed I'd been wrong to do so, since I'd made changes for a man who didn't want anything permanent with me, and a boy who wasn't mine to keep. I'd been a fool. And worse, I'd allowed myself to be hurt in the process.

Was it that Darius no longer wanted to be a primary caregiver to Peter? He worked long hours. It was the reason why he'd hired Gwen, a full-time nanny. Was it that he'd come to believe what his mother had told him? He should know his mother was wrong. Peter needed to be here with him, not off at boarding school. He needed Darius's presence, and it didn't matter how many late nights Darius worked; it only mattered to Peter that he was with him.

What was I thinking? Of course, Darius knew that. This had to be Helen. Obviously, Helen had contacted the school and given them Darius's information. She was the one who had been pushing for Peter to go to the exclusive boarding school. Darius had shot it down. This was more of Helen's manipulating.

I felt a rush of relief as I realized this had his mother's

handprint all over it. Darius would be home in a few hours and I would ask him then. But already, I felt peace taking over, where before there had been concern and that sick feeling of having been blindsided. Again.

CHAPTER 31

DARIUS

Hope was standing in the kitchen, watching Pete and Gwen playing on the carpet in the living room. The sadness on her face had uneasiness cracking me wide open. I'd done the one thing I'd never meant to do - make Hope unhappy.

"Are you all right?" I asked tentatively, resting my hands against the island.

She nodded, but she didn't meet my eyes. "You got a call on the landline today. From Kingsley Academy for Boys. They want you to call them about your application."

I sighed as realization dawned. "Thank you."

"Thank you?" Now she looked at me, her eyes brimming with tears. "You knew about the application?"

I nodded. "Yes. I got a text notification earlier today that they were reviewing the application. My mother must have listed both my numbers on the application when she submitted it. I have no idea why she didn't put her contact information, unless she means for me to know what she's done."

The tension went out of Hope's shoulders. "I knew she was behind this."

"I'm considering it."

"What? Why? Why would you do that?"

"It's a viable option."

"A viable option? He's just a kid. He needs you in his life. Boarding school would be a mistake. You've said so yourself."

"I'm not so sure anymore," I commented calmly. "It would provide a structure in his life that I currently can't. Gemini Inc. demands so much of me. I can't be here for Peter the way I should be."

"That's nonsense. That's your mother's biased opinion talking. You can't believe that."

There was a sour taste in my mouth, but I continued anyway. "I can only go with what I know. I'm hiring nannies to care for him. He had an allergic reaction and ended up in the hospital. That could have been so much worse than what it turned out to be."

"That wasn't your fault. Even two-parent households face situations like that with their children."

"Look at how many long hours I'm working? Look at you. You're always having to leave late. And Gwen's about to face the same thing. Right now, Pete's only four, but what happens when he gets older and begins to notice how much I'm gone."

"Then hire more help at your office." She sighed, closing her eyes. She took a deep breath before she continued. "He'll really notice your absence if you put him in boarding school." She reached across the island and placed her hand over mine. "Come on, Darius. You're being too hard on yourself."

I shook my head and pulled my hand away. I folded my

arms over my chest and did my best to ignore the hurt look in her eyes.

"I'm not equipped to handle this."

"So, you're just giving up? Sending him away?"

"I'm giving him a better option."

"In which world is boarding school a better option for a four-year-old?"

"Mine."

"You don't believe that. What would Shawn and Alice say to you right now?"

"They aren't here." It hurt like hell to say it, but it was the truth. They weren't here. I was, and I could only do the best job I could do.

A dull ache started at the nape of my neck. I rubbed my palm over the achy spot, hoping to ease the pain. I knew she would object when she found out about the application, and I thought I'd braced myself to explain to her why I wasn't putting an end to it. But I wasn't prepared to argue with Hope. I never wanted to be the one to cause her pain, but I could see that this conversation was hurting her.

I'd thought this over all day. Boarding school wasn't the best, but it was a better option than me.

"I've thought about it, Hope. I think it's for the best."

She stared at me; her face grim. I saw the hurt and disappointment in her eyes. Finally, she shook her head.

"I can't do this. I have to go."

I watched her turn and walk out of the kitchen. A protest started on my lips but died there. While there was a part of me that wanted to stop her, the more sensible part that wanted the best for Hope knew that her walking away from me was the best thing for her.

I braced my hands against the kitchen island and took a deep breath, hoping to dull the ache in my chest. In the end, I had very little to offer Hope, and my business would always demand more from me. I knew she desired more than what we currently had. She deserved it all: an attentive husband, children of her own. She thought she could settle for me. But she would only end up alone and frustrated, waiting for me and always feeling like the second best. I couldn't put Hope through that. Just as I couldn't put Peter through that either.

I wiped my wet eyes with my fingers and took another calming breath. I loved her. More than I loved Gemini or Peter or anyone else. I loved her enough to want what was best for her, even if it wasn't the best for me. That meant letting her walk away.

CHAPTER 32

HOPE

"Hello, Hope."

I turned at the sound of his voice. He looked tall standing in my doorway. His broad shoulders almost filled the entire entryway to my classroom.

"Johnathan. What are you doing here?" I set the books I'd been packing away down on my desk.

"Happy New Year."

"Happy New Year to you too."

"I wanted to see how you were doing."

"I'm fine. Getting ready for the new school year."

His gaze roamed over my face and down my body. I knew what he saw. An oversized sweater and jeans that were a little loose. Five days after walking out on Darius and Peter, my appetite was still non-existent, but hey, I'd lost that stubborn five pounds, so there was that.

"You look like crap." He took a step into the room. "You've got circles under your eyes. Are you sleeping?"

"I'm fine. What do you want?"

"I still care about you. I haven't changed my mind about wanting to be with you, in spite of what's happened these last months."

I shook my head. "I haven't changed my mind."

"Hope, for God's sake. Wake up. I don't know what it is you're expecting to find out there. We were good together."

"Why? Because you worked late at the office screwing the boss's daughter? Because I hung around longer than I should have? Why were we good together, Johnathan? I told you. I'm not interested in a relationship with you."

"Because of him?"

"Because of you, Johnathan."

"I've changed."

"I haven't. And you and I were never a good fit to begin with. Please don't make this any more difficult than it already is. You have my answer. I'm not changing it."

"You're making a mistake, being so choosy, so demanding. You're going to end up alone. Is that what you want?"

I felt the fear and let it wash over me. He was talking about my worst nightmare. It was the thing I feared the most. But even as I tasted the fear, I felt the burst of peace chase it away, like the sun peeping through the morning clouds.

"I would rather be alone the rest of my life than settle because I was afraid. I'm not settling, Johnathan. Not for the leftovers that a man decides to throw my way. I deserve more than that. I may never get it. You're right. I might end up alone. But at least I know that I wouldn't have compromised what I hoped for—dreamed of—my entire life."

"You're making a mistake."

"Then it'll be mine to regret. Goodbye, Johnathan."

I watched as he turned and walked away without another word. My legs felt weak beneath me. Sitting in my chair, I stared at my desk. I'd given up something less for the belief in something that was going to be worth it. Had I made a mistake? Was I being too idealistic?

Maybe.

Could I settle for the alternative?

Absolutely not! Growing bitter and regretting that I hadn't held out for what would make me truly happy was more than I was willing to bear. I wanted commitment and romance and a marriage, but I needed love too. I didn't want to settle for a life without love.

It was why I'd walked out on Darius a week ago, and I hadn't gone back, not even to get my things. It hurt that he hadn't followed me, or called me, or even dropped by my classroom just to say hi. He'd let me go so easily. I understood now that as magical as our Christmas holiday had been, it hadn't been permanent, and perhaps that was what Darius had wanted.

I missed Peter just as I knew I would. I was hopeful that I would see him in my class in a couple days when school started. But I was equally worried that Darius had followed through with his decision to send Peter to that boarding school.

I couldn't convince him that he was better for Peter than he was giving himself credit for. He was so stubborn, believing that there was better out there than him. He didn't see himself the way Peter and I did. And he wasn't listening to me.

I got to my feet and picked up the textbooks off my desk. Walking over to the bookshelf in the corner, I stacked them there, ready for the eager little hands that would discover them. I'd done the right thing walking away from Darius. I just wish it didn't hurt so much.

CHAPTER 33

DARIUS

The office was quiet, everyone having left hours ago. I ignored the niggling feeling that I should have left with them and focused on the plans spread out in front of me on my work desk. Outside, it was already dark, and when I glanced out the window, all I saw was my reflection and the interior of my empty office.

Two weeks had passed since Hope had walked out of my house, leaving Peter and me alone. Two weeks of non-stop thinking about her. Missing her. Two weeks of wondering if I'd done the right thing by not fighting for her and feeling that cold, clammy feeling that I'd made a mistake.

Being with Hope had been the best time of my life. Caring for Peter with her at my side had seemed easy, effortless. She would make a great mother one day. She was already a terrific teacher. Peter had opened up and really come into his own under her care. Even now, he was doing well with Gwen, even if he did miss Hope and asked for her often. At first, I'd told him he would see her again when he went back to school, then once I'd made the final decision to put him in boarding school, I'd just stopped promising him that he would see her again altogether.

At least Peter was doing okay in spite of Hope's absence. Thank God he hadn't sunk into a depression. Gwen had a lot to do with it. He'd transitioned well from Hope caring for him to Gwen's presence during the day.

I was grateful for Gwen and the steady care she provided Peter. Soon, however, Peter would be at Kingsley and then her care for him would only be on weekends when he flew home.

A quiver of unease shimmied up my spine, and I pushed away from my desk to stand at my window. I leaned my forearm against the glass window and pressed my forehead against my arm. It was so dark outside I could only see my face staring back at me in the window.

What the fuck was I doing?

I couldn't send Peter to Kingsley. I couldn't go through with it.

I kept telling myself I was making the right decision by putting Peter in a boarding school just during the week and flying him home for weekends with me. His week would have more structure and I could carry along on my life's path before the accident; before Peter came to live with me. But the more I thought about it, the sicker I felt inside.

I needed Peter as much as he needed me. I loved tucking him into bed at night or checking in on him when he was already asleep. Sure, it was tiring and sometimes he tried my patience and I longed for a night out with the guys. Sometimes I felt torn wanting to be with him and needing to work late at the same time, and I hated that feeling of being torn and unable to fix it. But sending him to a boarding school wasn't going to fix any of that. In fact, I was making a bigger mistake by sending him away. I'd never be able to live with myself.

I'd let my mother and my circumstances wear me down into considering the one thing I'd sworn I wouldn't do when it came to Peter: send him away. I'd come up with all these reasons why it was the best thing for him. Truthfully, I was just being a coward.

Fear.

I'd let my fear steer me toward a decision that I had been dead set against. Fear of all the ways I would fail Peter, and of all the things I couldn't give him had me falling in line with my mother's plan. I'd been a fool. I knew firsthand that the negatives of sending him away far outweighed the benefits. I didn't need Peter to be groomed for the business world. I would teach him whatever he needed to know. And in the end, he would become whatever he wanted to become. If he chose to come into the business, I would make sure he was prepared for it. And if he chose to do something else? Well, that would be wonderful too, and I would move heaven and earth to help him succeed at whatever he wanted to do.

I'd allowed my fear of losing Peter, and my fear of me not being good enough to care for him, push me into a bad decision. Now that I could breathe again, I knew I didn't have the fortitude to go through with it. I would never turn my back on him.

Hope.

My breath fogged the glass in front of me. I'd failed her too. I'd pulled away from her, letting her walk out of my life when I never should have.

My fear of failing with Hope, of Hope ending up despising me for all my shortcomings and of us losing our relationship had caused me to end things with her when I should have been telling her that I wanted more than a friendship with her, or causal lovemaking. I had let fear make my decisions for me, and now here I was at the office, completely miserable.

I wanted to be on my way home to Hope and Peter and our dinner time routine. I wanted to be making love with her after we'd put Peter down for the night. Instead, it had been weeks since I'd seen her. And I was afraid that she never wanted to see me again.

"Hey, you okay?"

I jumped at the unexpected voice and turned around to find Hayden standing just inside my doorway.

"Yeah. What are you still doing here?"

"I could ask you the same thing. Everything all right?"

I released my pent up breath and walked over to my desk. Pulling my chair out, I sat down at my computer and shook my mouse. My computer whirled to life. I didn't want to lie to Hayden, but I wasn't sure I could admit the truth to him either.

"It's been a long day," I admitted.

"So, why aren't you home with Peter, and what's the new nanny's name, Gwen?"

Irritation surfaced and I shot him a look of annoyance. "Yes, her name is Gwen. Why would I be home with her?"

He shrugged. Walking over to my desk, he picked up my baseball and started tossing it back and forth.

"Dunno, man. I thought you were hot for Hope, but then you replaced her with Gwen. I'm just trying to keep up."

"You're being a dick, and you know it."

Hayden chuckled. He sat in the chair in front of me. "So, what happened between you two anyway?"

"Why would I tell you? So you could make fun of me?"

"I'm just trying to understand what went wrong."

I sighed and met his gaze across my desk. What could I tell him? The truth? That I'd let fear self-sabotage my relationship with Hope? That I'd let my fear enroll my four-year-old nephew in a boarding school?

"Not sure myself."

"Do you love her?"

I heard his question and I felt my answer all the way to my soul. I knew it in the way my heart skidded to a stop before correcting its rhythm. I felt it in the heat rushing under my skin. Yes. I loved Hope. I would probably love her for an eternity. I was always going to root for her. There was nothing I wouldn't do for her. If she needed me, or anything from me, I would give it to her. I owed her for life. And I would love her for the rest of mine, with all my heart.

"Yes," I whispered.

"You do?" Hayden spoke softly. "Jeez, man. What are you doing? Letting her walk away?"

"You're one to talk!" I sat back in my chair and eyed Hayden.

"You're right. My track record sucks. I've seen enough shit-shows to know that you don't let the real thing pass you by."

"It's not that simple."

"Life is short." He looked me in the eye as he said it. I frowned. It was something I used to say a lot, following Shawn and Alice's death. I'd stopped saying it lately, but it didn't change the fact that it was still true.

Had I forgotten that? Had I stopped taking the chances I knew I should take, because I was letting fear stop me when I should do it anyway because there were no guarantees in life?

What the hell was I doing? Was I letting fear of what could go wrong between Hope and me stop me from going after what I really wanted: a life with Hope?

"What changed?"

Fear.

Shawn and Alice's death had been the worst possible thing that could ever have happened to me. Or so I'd thought. Then Hope had walked into my life and I'd begun falling in love with her. I knew that even the tragedy of losing my brother and his wife paled in comparison to how I would feel if I loved Hope and lost her. How would I survive that? It had seemed easy to let her walk away.

Or so I'd thought. These past couple weeks had proven I absolutely needed Hope in my life. I was a mess without her. I loved her and being apart from her was like being underwater without air. Painful. It hurt. The worse part was I had the power to stop it. But I was too much of a coward. So, here I was, stuck on a merry-go-round of emotions that I just couldn't get out of.

"She's probably better off without me."

"Maybe, but you don't know that for sure. And you're certainly not better off without her."

That was true. I wasn't.

"What would Shawn have done?"

"What?"

"If he knew how he and Alice would end, do you think he would have done anything different? You're letting fear stop you from even trying. What if the tables were turned, and you'd died, and Shawn had taken in your son and met Alice? Do you think he would let her go? Or would he have fought to make a life with her? Wasn't he already doing that?"

Hayden was right. Shawn had fought to make it work with Alice, even going against his nature and choosing her over his ambition for more in business.

"So, here's another way of looking at it: knowing how difficult its been to scale Gemini, would you still have partnered with us? Or if you had to do it all over again, would you tell the three of us to shove it?"

I'd been a fool. I'd let my fear hold me back from committing to Hope when I should have dived headfirst into a relationship with her. I'd made a mistake by not going after her. I had no idea if she would give me another chance, but I needed to find out.

"When did you get so smart?" I asked Hayden as I stood.

He rose to his feet too. "You can't be the only one who matures out of this."

I grabbed my suit jacket off the back of my chair and pulled it on. "Thank you, Hayden. You've been a great friend. I appreciate your advice."

"You're welcome. What are you going to do?"

"I'm going to get Hope."

I left my office, walking down the deserted hallway toward the elevators. I wanted to head over to Hope's apartment, but I drove toward McKnight Grove instead. I had to get Peter. He was missing Hope as much as I was and the two of us were a packaged deal. Hope knew it, and I suspected she liked us that way, but if I was going after her, I needed to be sure. I needed Peter with me.

Momentary panic that I was making a fool of myself and I was going to end up heartbroken had my foot easing off the gas pedal. But I shook the fear away, convinced that I had to try. I needed Hope in my life.

CHAPTER 34

HOPE

I was about to sit down to watch *The Prince's Christmas Wish* again on my parents' new flat-screen tv, when the front doorbell rang. Who in the world could be ringing their doorbell so late at night? They were both already upstairs in bed. I set my bowl of popcorn and the remote control down on the coffee table and went to answer the door.

I looked through the peephole and felt my heart drop into my stomach. When I pulled the door open, Darius's eyes widened at the sight of me.

I held on to the open door. The sight of Darius and Peter standing there left me feeling as though I had been plunged into a cold pool of water. No, rather, I felt like the drop of water being swallowed whole by the ocean.

"What are you doing here?" My voice was barely a whisper. It lacked the vigor, anger, or fierceness it ought to have at the sight of my ex-lover and his ward on my parents' doorstep late at night.

"I came to ask your mom for your address. I needed to speak to you."

He still wore his suit pants with a white shirt, though he'd lost the tie and the jacket. Peter was already dressed in his pajamas, standing next to Darius, holding his hand with a Lego jet in his other.

"May we come in?"

I glanced over my shoulder. My parents were still upstairs. I stepped aside to let them in. Closing the door behind them, I leaned against it to catch my bearings.

Three weeks since I'd last seen him, but my heart still fluttered in my chest at the sight of him standing in front of me. Three weeks since I'd walked away from him, but I still longed to feel his arms around me. I still wanted his mouth on mine.

"Darius? What are you doing here?"

He rubbed the back of his neck, his hand falling by his side.

"I miss you," he finally spoke. "We both do." His voice was soft, firm, coaxing, like a trainer working with a wary animal.

"You miss me?" I questioned. "Has something happened to Gwen?"

"No, she's fine. She and Pete are getting along great. Right, Pete?"

Pete nodded, then pulled his hand away from Darius's and closed the distance between us, wrapping his arms around my legs. My heart squeezed before expanding completely with love for him, like a balloon taking in helium.

I bent down and picked him up. He smelled like his baby powder-scented shampoo. He rested his head on my shoulders, both his little arms going around my neck.

"But, Hope," Darius continued, drawing my gaze back to him as he took a step toward us. "Gwen's not you. And Peter and I both miss you a lot."

My heart raced as if I were a horse in the Kentucky Derby coming out of the gates.

"I don't understand." I shifted from one foot to the other, holding Peter tightly in my arms.

"I was wrong to let you walk away."

The tightness in my chest loosened, but I still felt breathless.

"It's been lonely without you these past weeks. I miss your voice, your touch. I miss our conversations. You're the one I want to come home to, Hope, and it's not been the same without you."

He was describing how I felt. "I miss you too. Both of you."

He reached out his hand to cup my cheek, and I let him because I needed his touch as much as I needed oxygen.

I was in love with Darius.

I was head over heels, happy-like-a-jolly Santa in love with Darius. But I couldn't settle for a causal relationship, even though being away from him these past three weeks had felt like slowly dying inside.

"I love you."

His face went blurry in front of me. I blinked, and the tears fell. He was so close to me I could see the golden flecks in his beautiful eyes.

"I love you too, both of you." I took a deep breath and swallowed. "But, Darius, love isn't the issue between us, is it?"

He took another step toward Peter and me. His lips were so close to mine. My gaze fell to his mouth, and my heart fluttered at the slow smile easing them apart.

"No." He shook his head. "It isn't. I know that." He lifted his other hand to my face so that he was holding me.

"But I do love you," he continued. "I think I started falling in love with you from day one. You made me feel alive again. The thing is, I only wanted to feel alive with you. I wanted to be with you. You're the only woman who's made me want to be better than what I am. Want more than what I have. I don't want to do this without you by my side."

I closed my eyes and shook my head. "I can't handle you shutting me out. Or choosing your work over me. I don't want to hold you back. What if one day you decide that you needed someone better?"

"There is no one better than you."

"I love what we had, but I want more –"

"You deserve more." He cut me off. I stared at him past my tears. "I want to give you so much more. I should have told you so when I took you to bed." I looked down at Peter, but he was oblivious to our conversation, his head still on my shoulder.

Darius continued, "I should have told you that I want you in every area of my life and my home and I don't want to have to hide that. Hope, I should have told you so many things a long time ago. But I let my fear hold me back."

"Your fear?"

"Yes. I was afraid of losing you. I'm still afraid of that. I'm afraid of losing you. I'm afraid I'll do something that messes everything up. I'll get busy at the office and skip our dinner plans. Or choose work over you and Peter or something, and I'll do something that annoys you. I've let my fear keep me from doing what I really want to do. What I should have done a long time ago."

"What?"

"Choose you, Hope. You. Peter. A little girl who looks exactly like you. I want those things with you. And, yes, I want Gemini too. I want it all. I know I can have it. If you'll give me another chance with you, I promise, you wouldn't regret it."

"Another chance?"

He nodded. "I wanted to find you tonight to ask you a very important question."

I laughed. "And what is that exactly?"

"Will you marry me?"

Adjusting Peter on my hip, I hooked an arm around Darius's neck and pulled him the last few inches toward my lips. The roaring in my ear sounded a lot like clapping.

I pulled back to see my mom and dad standing on the staircase, smiles on their faces. They must have heard us talking and come downstairs to see what was going on.

"Is that a yes?" Darius smiled.

"Yes." I laughed. "A thousand times, yes."

CHAPTER 35

DARIUS

ONE YEAR LATER

The afternoon sunlight shone down on the gardens of the McKnight Grove Country Club, chasing the late December chill away. Heating lamps stood at both ends of each row of chairs. They lined the aisle, radiating their warmth over the red carpet that was covered with white rose petals.

Excitement permeated the air. A small crowd sat in white covered chairs, beaming at me. It crackled like electricity bouncing around the gardens, from the back near the building to the front, where I stood with Peter and the pastor beneath a wooden gazebo covered in rose vines, waiting for the love of my life to walk down the aisle with her father and take my hand in marriage.

Anticipation crawled along my spine. We were finally

doing it. One year after asking Hope to be my wife, the day had finally come when she did. We were gathered here before our family, reminding me of the momentous decision I'd made to take a step away from fear and toward the promise I saw with Hope every day.

So much had happened in the twelve months since I'd impulsively gone to her parents' house to get her home address, not expecting her to answer the door. It had been perfect. I'd asked her to take me back as her husband and she'd said yes.

Sometimes, especially when I was tired, the questions about whether our relationship would last, if we could parent Peter and give him everything he needed, and whether I could still feed the beast that was Gemini Inc. and continue our company's growth, sneaked up on me. Despite those questions, I felt strongly that I needed Hope in my life. She was my heart, and I was lost in this world without her.

Late at night, after Peter went down to bed, when I took her to bed and we made love, everything, including all those questions, faded away.

The wedding march began, and everyone turned around to see her standing there with Lorenzo. My vision blurred. I swiped at my eyes. Hope was beautiful. Her long black hair fell in waves around her bare shoulders. Her strapless gown hugged her chest and torso before swaying over her hips and falling like a waterfall down her legs. She was hot, and I wanted to walk down the aisle and carry her away. Only the desire to have her be mine permanently kept me standing in place, waiting for her.

"You look amazing!" I murmured to her when she finally stood in front of me. I held out my hand, and she slipped hers into mine.

I nodded to her dad, who left her standing there with me, and took his seat in the front row next to her mom. Across the aisle, Hayden gave me the thumbs-up. Brian, who was sitting between Hayden and Gwen, smiled and nodded.

We turned our attention to the pastor. His words filled the gardens and wrapped around Hope and me.

"Dearly beloved, we have come together in the presence of God to witness and bless the joining together of Darius Peyton and Hope Martinez. The two have declared a desire to be joined as one in love and marriage."

Our friends and family cheered in agreement. The pastor continued, saying a lot of other things that all faded in comparison to Hope's beautiful face smiling up at me.

"With the powers invested in me by the State of Texas, I now pronounce you husband and wife. Darius, you may kiss your bride."

I pulled Hope into my arms and lowered my lips over hers. She tasted of strawberries and champagne. I kissed her like no one was watching. I put every promise I'd ever made to her, every dream I had for us into that kiss. I wanted her to know that I loved her, and that I was hers completely. Now and for a lifetime.

Life didn't make me any promises. Shit could hit the fan at any moment. I couldn't let fear of the unknown hold me back, though. I didn't want Peter to grow up being held back by fear. So, it meant I had to lead him by example. I was done letting fear stop me from reaching for what I wanted in life. And what I wanted more than anything else was Hope.

I knew with my entire being that Hope and I were going to have the type of marriage that Lorenzo and Beth had: long-lasting and filled with love. We would make a great team, like Shawn and Alice had. I believed it with all my heart, and because I believed it, I knew it would be so.

EPILOGUE

HOPE

THREE YEARS LATER

"That's the one!" I exclaimed, pointing at the giant Christmas tree a few feet away that was entirely too big for the top of my Range Rover. Peter ran over to it, craning his neck to look up the length of the tree.

"It's huge!" Peter exclaimed.

"That it is." Darius shook his head and ran his hand through the hair at the nape of his neck. "Babe, I'm not sure about this one."

"Come on. That's what you said last year and look at how much fun we had decorating it."

He reached for my hand, and when I slipped mine into his, he pulled me closer to him. He rested his palm flat against my stomach, and tender love flowed through me at his touch. Bending down, he pressed his lips to mine briefly.

"Things are different this year. No way are you climbing the ladder to trim this tree. We should get something smaller, more manageable."

I placed my hand over his on my stomach, even as I stood on tippy toes to kiss his soft lips again.

"You're so sweet. I'm four months pregnant, not crippled. It'll be fine."

But he didn't budge. Darius had been growing more and more protective since the day we found out that we were expecting. I should be irritated by his constant hovering, but it only warmed my heart. He wanted the baby and me safe, and he was determined to keep us that way.

"Okay, how about we get this tree, but I'll decorate the bottom half with Peter, and you can climb the ladder to do the top."

"Promise?" He lifted an eyebrow at me.

"Yes, I promise. The last thing I want to do is anything that would jeopardize our baby."

"Okay. Deal."

We waited by the tree until we caught the eye of one of the attendants walking by. Only after we'd completed the purchase and arranged for the delivery did the three of us walk away from it.

"How about hot chocolate?"

"Yes!" Peter ran ahead of us, heading for the coffee truck parked a few feet away.

"Sounds wonderful." Darius draped his hand over my shoulders and pulled me closer against the side of his body.

I remembered our first Christmas together. We'd both been unsure then of how things would turn out with Peter. Johnathan had been a constant thorn in my side. And Darius and I had yet to give in to the desire between us. How far we'd come in three years. I liked to think it was because we had two wonderful guardian angels looking out for us.

Darius and I were happily in love. Beyond happy. We had a wonderful marriage filled with romance, hot sex, and companionship. To think we'd almost let fear stop us from reaching for what we both wanted. Darius and his two business partners were killing it in their industry. So much so that Darius had hired an executive assistant with a background in real estate development to help him with his workload. Gemini Inc. had six major projects this year, something they couldn't have imagined three years ago. They were over the moon and having to scale quickly in order to accept all of the job requests coming their way.

Meanwhile I was happy teaching at Silsbee Academy. I got to do the thing I loved most in the world. Other than caring for Darius and Peter of course. And soon, a new baby! We were over the moon.

Peter was doing great at Silsbee Academy too. Best of all, as his stepmom, I got to see him blossom every day into the wonderful young boy that Alice and Shawn would have been proud of.

"You're deep in thought," Darius whispered in my ear as we stood in line for hot chocolate.

"I'm just feeling blessed. Everything worked out, didn't it?"

"It did." Darius's lips on mine still had the power to weaken my knees.

"I'm so glad I asked you to be Pete's nanny for the Christmas holidays."

"I'm so happy I said yes."

"Not happier than I am."

"Let's agree, it's a draw."

"Let's."

I laughed as he lowered his lips to mine again. Three Christmases ago, I'd taken a chance on a heartbroken man and a sad little boy, only to have my heart come alive with their love. I would forever be grateful. The three of us were a family now. Soon to be a family of four. I'd waited for a relationship with good bones. I was glad I had.

THANK YOU

Thank you for reading *Falling For The Nanny!*

I hope you enjoyed Darius and Hope's story. Please consider leaving an honest review on Amazon and/or Goodreads.

Rafe, Brian and Hayden will have their own stories soon.

If you'll like to be notified about my upcoming releases, as well as what's happening with me, please visit my website and sign up for my newsletter: www.kayknolls.com.

ALSO BY KAY KNOLLS

LOVE WORTH HAVING

EVAN

The bass in the music sent vibrations up my legs, through my body, and out to my fingertips, which were holding the glass full of scotch I'd been nursing all night. I was leaning over the railing on the second floor, watching the countless bodies below me jumping to the sound of Chris Brown's "Turn up the Music." Behind me, Nate and Ty were each dancing with girls they'd pulled from the pit down below and brought up to the VIP section.

Tonight was guys' night out. Normally that meant poker at my place, but Ty had wanted us to experience the latest club he'd invested in.

From my current vantage point, I could see the dance floor, the high-top tables spaced around the room, the bar area swarming with people, and the front entrance. Every so often, the doors opened, and more people walked in. Ty's latest venture was a success. Club Yes was pulsing tonight.

As if on cue, the front doors opened again, and three girls walked in. A tingle of excitement raced up my spine. I straightened to my full six foot four inches and watched as Bryan, Ty's business partner, walked up to the three ladies and hugged one of them before shaking hands with the other two. He spoke to the one he'd hugged before calling Tammy, the hostess for the second floor VIP section, and turning them over to her.

Excitement coursed through my body as I watched Tammy lead the ladies around the perimeter of the first floor and over to the stairs leading up to me. I tensed as a man stepped in front of the one who'd stolen my breath. Even from this distance, I saw the slow smile that spread across her lips before she shook her head and sidestepped the man, catching up to Tammy and her self-assured friend who was dancing her way through the crowd. Relief replaced the tension coiling beneath my skin. I glanced at the tall brunette with legs that went on for days who followed the other two like a lamb to the slaughter before I once again focused on the one who had stolen my breath the minute she'd walked through the restaurant earlier tonight.

Our gazes had connected at that restaurant, and I'd seriously lost my train of thought. Thinking had been overrated as I'd watched her glide across the room toward me. Hell, breathing had been overrated. Only, she hadn't been coming toward me and the boys. Moments after she'd sat down, giving me her back, I'd still been staring at her like a deer caught in headlights.

Kind of like I was now. I twisted my body so that my back was to the railing as Tammy indicated the large sitting area directly across from ours. The one who was obviously leading tonight slid across the padded bench, loudly ordering a scotch as she went. Her request reminded me of the glass I was holding. I lifted it to my lips and took a sip of the smooth liquid while continuing to watch the woman who made everyone else around her pale in comparison. She smiled her thanks to Tammy and was in the process of sitting when she saw me.

I felt the one-two thump in my stomach even as she grabbed onto the table to steady herself. Hm, interesting. Did she also feel the pull of attraction between us? Then her model of a friend slid in next to her.

"Hey, you guys were at the restaurant tonight," Ty, who had been dancing in the space between the two sitting areas, suddenly announced.

Nate looked up from the blonde whose neck he'd been nuzzling as he grinded against her ass. He stopped dancing altogether and, pulling away from the blonde, walked over to the girls' table.

"Hey!" The irritated blonde stood there, her mouth hanging open, her hands on her waist. When she saw that she'd lost Nate's attention, she grabbed her friend's arm and they flounced away.

I felt a rush of irritation at my teammate's crass behavior. Nate was too self-absorbed to realize he'd just lost major points with two out of the three women at the table he'd approached.

"Yeah, so were you," Miss Self-Assured stated. The other two were watching in silence, in a way that indicated that they were just wing-women and this was all her show.

"Wanna dance?" Nate leaned down and held his hand out.

She stared at his outstretched hand for a couple beats before she slipped her smaller one into his. "I could dance."

Nate pulled her up from the bench and wrapped his arm around her waist. They started moving to the beat.

A minute later, Ty leaned down and whispered in the supermodel's ear. She nodded, though not as enthusiastically as her friend had accepted Nate's invitation. She glanced at the showstopper, who made a shooing motion with her hand. Soon she was alone at the table.

I downed the remainder of my drink, needing the liquid courage before moving over to her. She watched me cross to her the way a tourist would watch a panther on a safari—with open interest just so long as the panther stayed on his side of the wilderness.

"Mind if I sit?"

I saw her eyes go wide before she shook her head. I slipped into the booth across from her and leaned against the padded back of the bench. She really was beautiful to look at.

"I'm Evan."

"Christina."

I murmured her name on my lips, liking the sound of it. Her eyes went wide again, and I couldn't help but wonder what they would look like if she were below me and I was making her come.

"You're beautiful," I said.

She winkled her nose as if I'd said something bad. "Thanks." There was no gratitude in the word. Was she playing coy? Or was it that it wasn't very original? Now that I thought about it, it probably hadn't been very original. No doubt every guy she met led with that fact. She was looking at her friends dancing with my friends.

I wasn't a very good dancer. I was better on the field than off. But the music was seriously jumping, and she was worth making a fool of myself for. "Wanna dance?"

"Not right now, but thanks."

"Wow," I muttered. Struck down! I frowned into my

empty glass. I set it down on the table, then I looked up and found her staring at me, her lips curling up. Great, she was finding amusement at my expense. Not very encouraging.

"It's not you," she suddenly said. "I worked a fourteen-hour shift today and my feet are killing me."

Grateful for the bone she'd thrown me, I asked, "What do you do?"

"I'm a nurse at Mass Memorial."

Really? Now it was my eyes that went wide. Mass Memorial was one of the philanthropies my family supported. It was also one of the best teaching hospitals in the Houston area. Brains and a bombshell body. Damn, she was hot.

"What about you? What do you do?"

Was she for real? I crocked my head to the side as confusion warred with suspicion. I watched my friends dancing with the two girls before focusing on the beauty in front of me again. Was I being punked? Was she setting me up?

First, we'd seen them at the restaurant, seated in the private area not far from our table. Now they were at the same club, in the VIP section no less, seated at the table across from us. Were these girls stalking us? She scowled at me suddenly, and I realized it was because I had been frowning at her this whole time.

"Sorry." I shook my head with a laugh.

She laughed too. It was a musical sound that tickled my chest. "That's okay. And don't bother answering. These questions are always loaded anyway. I mean what if you're in between jobs, or what if you just lost your job today? It's horrible having to answer the prerequisite getting-to-know-you questions, isn't it?"

I shrugged, but I took the out she gave me. I still wasn't sure if she honestly didn't know who I was or if she was just playing ignorant to gain points with me. "Can I get you a drink?"

She shook her head. "I'm at my limit." Then she looked over at her friends again.

Nate and Miss Self-Assured were grinding on each other like long-lost lovers. Ty's model kept a decent amount of space between them. She had a face and a body created for a man's fantasy, but there was something about her that reminded me of Char and brought out my protective side. From the way Ty was handling her, I was pretty sure my friend felt it too.

"Excuse me," the showstopper across from me suddenly said, jumping to her feet.

I stood too. "Where are you going?"

She didn't quite meet my eyes as she answered, "Bathroom."

I watched her to-die-for, leather-clad legs carry her away from me. Her model friend smiled apologetically to Ty before excusing herself and following her. She touched Miss Self-Assured as she walked by, and I watched as the other girl grabbed Nate's shirt, pulling him behind her as she followed her friends down the stairs.

Ty met my eyes for a split second before a grin the size of Montana spread across his lips, and he too was dashing off toward the stairs after the others.

"Fuck me," I muttered to myself before I followed. I was so out of my element. It felt like they were calling plays I wasn't familiar with. Meanwhile, in one of the hottest dance clubs in downtown Houston, the only girl I'd wanted to dance with in years had turned me down and walked away. While the rejection was refreshing, I couldn't tell if it was legitimate or all part of her playing hard to get. And now here I was chasing after her.

Well, technically, I was chasing after Ty, who was chasing after the model, who was chasing after my girl. Tomayto, tomahto. Either way you looked at it, I was way out of my element.

I'd agreed to come to the club with Ty and Nate. It hadn't crossed my mind that a girl at the club might hook my attention the way Christina had. Well, technically, she'd hooked my attention as she'd walked through the restaurant. Whatever. She had my attention. What now?

Nate and Miss Self-Assured soon found a spot not too far away from the restrooms and were back to dancing while they waited for Christina. Ty and Nadia stood at a bar close by, ordering drinks.

I leaned against the wall and waited for Christina to come out. Watching Nate and her friend dance made me want to feel Christina's body moving against mine. I hadn't come to the club tonight planning to hook up with anyone, but one look at Christina and desire was coursing through my blood. I was usually the cool one. Not even a wingman really. More like the designated driver. I wasn't one for hooking up with strangers. Hell, I wasn't one for hooking up period. Now, it was like four years of celibacy was driving me hard and one woman had ignited that storm—Christina. I didn't even know her last name.

She came out of the restroom then. Her eyes immediately found mine, and I saw them go wide with surprise. I could tell she hadn't expected me to follow her. Her eyes were so expressive. Almond-shaped and slanted like a cat's, they also broadcasted her emotions. I liked reading them. Her gaze flitted over to Miss Self-Assured, then to the model at the bar with Ty, before finding mine again. She approached me slowly, one heeled foot in front of the other. Her hips swayed with every step she took. She reminded me of a tigress, sleek and sensual. Her eyes held my gaze. There was an intensity in them that hadn't been there before.

She stopped mere inches from me. Her chest brushed

against mine. A trail of heat coursed down my chest and straight to my dormant dick. I felt myself stirring and pushed off from the wall, adjusting my hips so that I wasn't touching her. She lifted her eyes to meet mine. Her chin didn't come higher than my collarbone. She was probably about five foot two without the heels.

"I'm ready to dance, if you want to." Her voice was husky.

Did I want to? Oh yeah, I wanted to. I placed my hand on the small of her back, leading her over to the edge of the dance floor. She lifted her hands, placed them on my chest, and started moving to the music. She was a sensual dancer. More hip action than wild, flailing movements. I matched her moves easily, and I didn't feel like I was making a fool of myself. I liked the way she danced.

I caught the scent of vanilla and coconut and realized it was her hair. I lowered my nose to the side of her neck, stepping closer, and inhaled deeply. She smelled hot, like a decadent dessert I wanted to lick. Jesus! Four years of celibacy was about to go down the tubes tonight, and I didn't mind one bit.

Her hands trailed up my chest before looping around my neck. My hands tightened against her back and pulled her tighter against my chest. I didn't want her to feel the bulge in my pants. I didn't want to offend her, but hell, I needed to feel her against me.

The music tempo changed suddenly. An older, slower song came on. I recognized it from that dancing movie my mom watched when we were growing up. I tightened my arms around Christina and felt her sway against me as the male voice sang of the girl being like the wind. Christina was overpowering my senses. Her smell, the feel of her body against mine, her breath on my neck. She encapsulated me. I was lost in the storm that was Christina, and I didn't want to come up for air.

I lifted my head from her hair when I felt her steps falter. I pulled back far enough to look into her eyes. My heart slammed against my chest before settling somewhere in my stomach. I saw my emotions mirrored in her brown depths.

"I'm going to kiss you now," I warned her.

Her eyes flared in surprise. I watched her nibble on her lip before she nodded. Her tongue darted out to touch the full part of her lower lip. With a groan, I lowered my mouth to hers, capturing her lips, pulling her flat against my body. She parted her lips for me and let me play with her tongue. She tasted of scotch and mint. Delicious. She was delicious.

I felt the bass pumping again, but I didn't hurry our kiss. We stood still, locked together right there on the edge of the dance floor, lost in the world we were creating together.

The first kiss ended, and another began, and then another. I heard her moan and the sound shot straight to my groin. Everything faded to a dull roar. I felt light-headed. If she was willing, I was taking her home tonight. Rules be damned.

The flash of light behind my eyes was disorienting. Then it came again against my closed eyelids. This time, I stiffened. Even in my current distracted state, I recognized that flash. I lifted my head and was momentarily blinded by another flash. I angled my body so my back was to the photographer and Christina was hidden. Another flash. Christ! Where was security?

As if I'd conjured them up, I saw two bouncers moving toward the photographer. The photographer took one more picture and then darted around Christina and me, heading for the back exit. Moments later, the man pushed through the door and was gone.

"Is everything okay? What was that?"

I focused on Christina, realizing that I was still holding her against me. I dropped my arms and took a step back. I had a pretty good idea of the images the photographer had caught. They told a story all on their own. But when combined with the words from some two-bit tabloid press?

How had a simple night out turned so complicated so fast?

Buy LOVE WORTH HAVING now or
Read for free in Kindle Unlimited

ABOUT THE AUTHOR

Kay Knolls writes contemporary romances featuring alpha males and strong heroines in steamy, emotional situations that deliver all the feels, and always ends in a happily ever after!

Kay lives in Texas with her family. When she's not writing, she's usually reading a book, or at the beach, digging her toes in the sand.

Learn more about Kay on her website:
www.kayknolls.com
Social Media:
Facebook: facebook.com/authorkayknolls
Twitter: twitter.com/KayKnolls
Instagram: instagram.com/authorkayknolls
Bookbub: bookbub.com/profile/kay-knolls